APPALACHIAN TRAILS

A SMOKY MOUNTAIN MYSTERY

RUTH MCCOY

APPALACHIAN TRAILS

First Edition

For permission requests, contact Publisher:
Smoky Mountain Mysteries
TarheelLinda@gmail.com

Cover Design and Formatting by The Book Khaleesi
www.thebookkhaleesi.com

ISBN 978-0-578-93085-5 (paperback)

Printed in the United States of America
10 9 8 7 6 5 4 3 2 1

For Calvin and Mary

They shut the road through the woods
Seventy years ago.
Weather and rain have undone it again,
And now you would never know
There was once a road through the woods.

~ Rudyard Kipling ~

PROLOGUE

The young woman lay on her bed and stared at the ceiling. Her focus blurred as she lost herself in the past. She attempted to recall the events which led her to this day.

Earliest memories were filled with a montage of scenes with her family in a warm safe home, then of venturing into the world of Franklin with Sunday School and Vacation Bible School, Saturdays on Main Street to meet friends and shop.

As she grew, occasional weekend trips to Atlanta or Asheville indicated a greater world outside of Franklin but school and church centered her life. Popular at Franklin High School she was elected to be a cheerleader all four years; as a senior she was voted head cheerleader. Everyone admired her confidence and accomplishments. As friendships grew and friends claimed more of her time than family did, she grew increasingly independent with each passing day.

The mountains and forests were always there with a beckoning and menacing presence. They loomed over the edges of Franklin and, because she had been warned of their many dangers—snakes and bears, trails which led nowhere, storms that rolled abruptly over the ridges, she did not enter alone until she was in her teens. Even then she was cautious and preferred to go in the company of others.

Weekends she spent with friends hiking trails, canoeing on the river, hunting in the many mountain forests surrounding the valley, or fishing in the Little Tennessee River. The small town did not provide many activities for the town's teenagers. By the time she went to the University in Chapel Hill she was ready for a larger world.

The first year, the college atmosphere with its opportunities, that seemed unlimited, enthralled her with a sense of newness and adventure. Her life revolved around classes and her dorm. Sophomore year gave her the opportunity to live off campus and she shared a house on Rosemary Street with three friends. From there she could walk to campus with the student union and library, and also she had easy access to the restaurants, like the Carolina Coffee Shop, and bars, such as He's Not Here.

She had found her niche and she reveled in it.

CHAPTER

1

The red sky at morning warned of storms ahead. The mackerel sky predicted the storms would arrive that day. Daisy McLaren was not concerned about the weather. She had more immediate and important worries troubling her.

She drove by the exit her mother had used on the last day of her life and automatically turned to look. She did this each time she passed and wondered why her mother had died alone, on a deserted dirt-and-gravel mountain road—leaving Daisy motherless too soon.

She took the next exit off the Appalachian Parkway and traveled up Ruby Mine Road as the morning fog was lifting, leaving smoky remnants to drift among the high mountaintops. In the passenger seat, Jake Smith connected a microphone to his video camera. A plane had crashed on a remote mountain near Franklin, North Carolina. Daisy and Jake were going to film a report to send to WLOS in Asheville.

"Slow down, Daisy! The plane's not going anywhere."

A rescue squad fire engine came up behind them with lights on, but no siren. Daisy pulled over as far as she could to let it pass. Jake looked down on a rocky creek bed that seemed to be a thousand feet below. "Can't you get any closer?" he snarked.

"You turning green? I think there's a paper bag in the glove compartment if you need it."

Jake gave her a sharp glance.

"Next time I'm driving."

They continued up the paved road.

"Lights are on at the Simpsons' store. Guess the crash woke them up," Jake said.

"We can stop by on the way back. I want to get to the crash now. For once I want to be at the right place at the right time."

About a quarter mile beyond the Simpson Ruby Mine, the road switched back and forth around the cliff face. The uphill lane was on the edge and dropped steeply through oak and poplar to the road below. The deep green of the laurel thickets would keep through the approaching winter as the leaves on the deciduous trees turned to reds, yellows, and oranges. Daisy drove as fast as she dared. Another quarter mile on, the road turned into deeply rutted gravel and narrowed so much there was barely room for one car.

They were in a mountain forest, filled with both white and red oak trees, along with a scattering of tulip poplar and pines. Thickets of laurel, called ivy by the old timers, were interspersed among the trees.

Every so often there was a pull-off, an area built up and topped with gravel. Daisy hoped there would be one at the crash site, but there was none.

The fire engine and ambulance were on the road ahead, and the Macon County sheriff's car was behind them. Daisy stopped and put on the emergency brake. "You might have to get out on my side."

"Be there in a minute."

Daisy walked carefully by the vehicles to join the assembly of officials. She got out a notepad and pen and started writing. Her brain was engaged now. As was her custom, she began by describing the scene in front of her, the physical environs, and the vehicles.

She looked down on the old Cessna 172E below. The body of the plane was in one piece, but it had sheared one wing off. She could see the pilot slumped over and not moving. The door on the other side of the small craft seemed to have been thrown open on impact. The tail was intact, and she made a note of the Cessna's number.

Daisy noticed Lamar Bell as he prepared to descend to the plane. Lamar had been the captain of the football team when she was a cheerleader at Franklin High, and she had harbored a crush on him for a year even though it drove Jake crazy.

Jake could have played football. He had the sinewy strength that came from long hours of hard work, but because he had to work so hard to help his mom, he did not have time for sports. Sometimes Daisy had felt bad about teasing Jake, but she loved it too much to stop. Who else would she tease, if not her best friend?

She stopped writing as Lamar began his descent.

"Are you getting this, Jake?" She turned to see Jake following Lamar's movements with his camera.

In the stands of pine, a few scraggly rhododendrons stretched skyward seeking sunshine. Last fall's leaves carpeted the ground, still wet from recent rains, so, moving from tree to tree, Lamar proceeded cautiously down the steep incline.

When he reached the plane, he opened the cockpit door and looked inside. He turned, held up one finger, and shook his head. One person, dead. Lamar unfastened the seat belt of the pilot and dragged him out. The woods and laurel thickets were too dense for a stretcher, so he just set him down and went to the other side of the plane. Nothing there. Lamar began the slow ascent to the waiting crowd.

Jake filmed the preparations as the rescue squad brought out axes and gas-powered chain saws to clear a path to the dead pilot's body.

Daisy approached Sheriff Ben Williams, a tall man in his fifties, who had retired from the FBI and was last stationed in the field office in Raleigh. He had planned to teach history and do some trout fishing, but they soon drafted him to run for sheriff of Macon County.

"Mr. Williams?"

"Hello, Daisy," he said. "I should've known you'd get here fast."

"Do you have any idea what caused the crash? Or where it was going?"

"Not yet. Wish I did. Only thing I know is that he isn't a local," the sheriff said. "I'll give you details as soon as I can. Gotta go now. You take care."

Daisy nodded and looked around for Jake. He stood at the edge of the road and motioned for her to join him to film a segment. As she reached her spot, the Cessna exploded.

CHAPTER

2

The shock wave created by the explosion did not reach Daisy standing on the side of the road, but she instinctively recoiled and covered her head. Jake set his equipment down and rushed over to shield her, but the blast and the chaos caused by the blast were over almost as soon as they had begun. What was left of the small plane after the crash was now in flames, and the surrounding trees and bushes had either been cleared by the explosion or were in flames.

Daisy took several deep breaths to recover. She would have to process what had just happened later because now she wanted to get everything on film for her report. There was no time for panic. They had to get their work done until the emergency officials made them leave the scene.

"Did you get that?" Daisy said.

Jake was all business too, now. "Sure did! Let's start. Can you get back in position?"

"This is Daisy McLaren for WLOS News. I'm standing on a mountainside outside of Franklin, where we have just witnessed the explosion of a small aircraft that crashed earlier this morning off Ruby Mine Road. The pilot died on impact. There were no passengers.

"Currently investigators have no explanation for why the plane was flying in this remote area. More information at the News at Six. Of course, I'll be posting updates on Facebook and Twitter as I receive more information."

The explosion had scattered debris through the woods. Small fires sprang up but soon died out in the still-damp leaves on the forest floor. Daisy saw Jake already making another video of the scene below.

"I got some good footage. Ready to hit the road again? I don't know about you, but I could use some chow about now."

"I guess." Daisy frowned as she read over her notes. "I wonder why the plane didn't explode when it crashed. Why did it happen just now?"

"I'm sure you'll figure it out. Let's go."

Daisy put the pad and pen in her bag and turned to rejoin Jake. Suddenly she stopped and pointed down the mountain. A flash of green has caught her eye.

"Wait," she said, "what's that?"

Jake looked down where she was pointing.

"I don't see anything."

"There." Daisy saw movement in the thickets farther down the slope and said again, "It's another man! He's heading down the mountain."

"Where?"

Daisy searched the woods below but saw no more signs that there could be a person there.

"I lost him."

"Are you sure it was a man? Could it have been a deer?"

Daisy stared briefly at Jake and went back to get in the car. "Why do you always have to second guess me? You know as well as I do that any deer that might have been around here ran away as soon as the plane crashed, and they sure would not have returned with all the commotion. It was a man."

"How do you know it wasn't a woman?"

"The way he ran!"

"That's a very sexist attitude you're displaying."

Daisy ignored him and went to the Jeep. "Do you want a ride or not?"

Jake walked to the passenger side of the Jeep and climbed in. "My life is in your pretty hands."

CHAPTER 3

As they drove down the mountain toward the valley where they lived, Daisy was quiet. It was obvious to her that the man who ran from the plane had caused it to explode, but how? And, more importantly, why? She decided it was pointless to discuss the importance of this with Jake. She needed to ascertain as way to get more information about the people who lived on Ruby Mine Road.

An abandoned farm was situated in a clearing before the road climbed into the forest. Once teenagers from Daisy's school were reputed to have wild parties there but Daisy and Jake had never attended. That is, Jake went to one of the gatherings, decided it was not for him, and never went back. Now the house, barn, and other out-buildings were concealed with kudzu. A tarp meant to protect a leaky roof sagged with the weight of soggy leaves. Blaze orange "Posted" signs cluttered the property to warn hunters, scavengers, and local teens to keep out. Seeing the derelict homestead, Daisy remembered that Caleb and Jasmine Walker had been part of that crowd of teenagers.

She broke the silence by asking, "How much farther to the Walkers' cabin from the crash site?"

The Walker family's farm occupied the plateau at the top of Ruby Mine Road. Daisy had gone to school with the son Caleb until tenth grade, when he just quit coming. Sometimes she saw him with his father at the Walmart, but she had never seen his mother. Daisy knew his older sister Jasmine through cheerleading, but they had never been close. Jasmine and Daisy were as different as night and day. The wild crowd held no attraction for Daisy.

Daisy had always thought the whole Walker family was strange, and now she wondered whether they might have something to do with the plane crash. Could the plane have been attempting to land at their farm? She did not think that the field afforded enough room for a landing strip, but now she thought anything was possible.

Jake looked askance at her. "Two miles as the crow flies. Thirty minutes driving."

"I want to go back and see what they know. Don't you think it's suspicious that this crash happened so close to their place?"

"Not really, and I'm pretty certain you've got to edit the video if you're going to post it on your vlog—and send it to Asheville in time for the evening news. Also, my stomach is threatening to get violent if it doesn't get food soon."

Daisy knew he was right. This story could be the break that would get her noticed by WLOS, the Asheville station serving the North Carolina mountains. She had lived in Franklin since her graduation from the university in Chapel Hill, and the limited opportunities increasingly frustrated her in her small hometown. If she could make it to Asheville, the next step would be to Charlotte or Raleigh. She scowled.

"Whoa, you know that's not one of your best looks! We can come back later."

"Promise?"

"Promise," Jake said, then added, "When did I ever lie to you? Now take me to Burger King, please."

"You're kidding. Burger King?"

"Not a bit. I got an actual job to get to. Not everyone can live at home and have their daddy pay the bills."

Daisy tensed up. Her mother had died in the car accident during Daisy's senior year. Daisy had returned home after graduation rather than seeking more challenging full-time work in Raleigh or Charlotte. Time passed, and here she was, five years later, still in Franklin, living in a garage apartment behind Lucas McLaren's home.

Daisy had not confided to Jake or anyone else that the official reports on her mother's accident did not satisfy her. Lucas either ignored her questions or flat out refused to discuss her mother's death. If he did respond to her request, he simply said that he truly did not know. Daisy never believed him, and she was determined to discover the truth so she could move on.

"Sorry, darlin'," Jake said. "You know I'm really glad you're here."

Daisy pulled into the Burger King. It was the morning rush hour in Franklin. People drove an hour from the mountains that were northwest of town for work. There was no development between Franklin and Bryson City, and high school and college students filled the seasonal work opportunities. The drive to downtown was fast and silent. Jake scarfed down his breakfast sandwich.

While she left Franklin for college, Jake stayed on. He used an old Leica that he had picked up at an antique mall to photograph anything that caught his fancy. He developed quite a reputation and was asked to take photos for *Our State* and the Raleigh *News & Observer*. After taking classes at the local community college, he began a second and more stable career working in the mobile applications development department at Drake Enterprises. He had made quite a bit of money when the company decided to share profits that they reaped from a photography app he had designed. Raised to be prudent, Jake spent little of that money and continued to place it in a savings account.

Returning after graduation to join the staff of the *Franklin Free Press,* Daisy kept the relationship as just friends. She had a relationship in Chapel Hill with another journalism student that ended badly. She endured depression until she got an antidepressant prescription, which she still filled monthly. Since then, she was on guard and suspicious of men, and even kept Jake at arm's length.

"Now don't go out there without me!" Jake said, as he got out in front of the Drake offices.

She nodded. She waved him off and thought about the day ahead. She planned to go first to the office to edit and file her account of the plane crash and to post it online, and then she would plan how to approach the Walkers. Turning onto Depot Street, she headed to the office.

She had already decided to go back on the mountain by herself.

CHAPTER 4

The newspaper office was located in a small industrial area of Franklin, a part of town seldom seen by tourists. The locals and the summer people often passed by on the way to the new post office to get packages that would not fit in mailboxes, to stop mail for vacations, to have mail forwarded, and sometimes just to purchase stamps.

The one-story brick building which housed the newspaper was built in the Sixties. It had the bland façade shared by many low-budget interpretations of Mid-Century Modern buildings. Employees appreciated the ample parking in a side lot. Daisy parked and rushed inside.

Reporters, copy editors, and advertisement salespeople had desks filling most of the vast building. A steady hum of voices and fingers tapping computer keyboards filled the room. Two offices walled off with half-glass partitions housed the chief accountant and the editor-in-chief and owner, Chad Melbourne, an import from Atlanta.

"How long have I got for the print edition?" she asked as she ducked into the editor's office.

"No worries," he said. "We're working with Jake's photos now. They're very good. Just write up a 250-word cutline to explain them, and we're good to go."

Daisy frowned and sighed.

"Don't fret," Chad said. "We'll print a full follow-up for the weekend edition. Take your time and get the details. Okay? And see me before you leave."

She nodded and headed to her desk. Opening her laptop, she sat down and typed, "Just before sunrise this morning a small plane crashed into the woods above the Simpson Ruby Mine." She finished the rest in a few minutes and sent it to Chad. That was that.

Her cell chimed, announcing a call from Jake. She looked at it for a few seconds before answering. She really did not need a lecture on personal safety from Jake because she had already made up her mind what her next step would be. So many questions remained. Chief among them was the identity of the man who ran away. Daisy was certain he had caused the plane to explode. He ran downhill so she thought it possible that he was one of the three Simpson sons, but she suspected that it was Caleb Walker.

"Yes?" she said.

"That all you got for me, darlin'?" Jake laughed. "And just when I was going to offer to take you to lunch."

"Too busy."

"Well now, what did I do to get a cold shoulder?"

"Nothing." Daisy said.

Jake laughed again.

"I actually just wanted to make sure you got back okay from the crash."

"Well, I did, obviously."

"And that you're not doing anything crazy, like going back up there by yourself to check out the Walkers?"

"So now you think I'm stupid?" Daisy said.

"Now, wait a minute. No way I said that. Just that sometimes you do stu- foolish things. And for the record, I said 'crazy,' not stupid!"

"That's even more insulting! I've got to go. A deadline to meet. When will you have the film edit ready from this morning? I need to post it online."

"You'll have it by six," Jake said. "Do you want me to bring it to you at home?"

"Email it, please."

With that, Daisy hung up. No way was Jacob Smith going to tell her what to do. She put her laptop in its case, grabbed her bag, and went to talk with Chad.

"I'm going back up to the crash site to see if I can spot anything I might have missed," she said. "It'll take a few days for the formal investigation to be completed. They will probably send the body to Raleigh for the post-mortem, so that will take a few days. The tox report will take even longer."

"What do you think you'll be able to see now that you couldn't a few hours ago?" Chad said.

"Not sure, but you never know. I don't have anything else until the school board meeting tonight."

"Have you done the feature I asked for about Hernando de Soto and his connection with a Cherokee princess and Franklin?"

"Working on it."

Chad drew a paper from the jumble of pages on his desk. "Well, look. I also need you and Jake to be ready to report on the aftermath of a tropical storm headed our way. It should reach us this evening."

Daisy studied the sheet. The year had been a bad one for storms, and most of them had traveled through the Caribbean to make landfall in the Southern states, Louisiana in particular. Macon County had accumulated enormous amounts of rain from these, but never excessive wind damage.

Chad continued, "Okay? And before you go, I want to notify you that next month we'll be cutting back on the print edition. Going to one paper on Wednesday."

"Why?"

"Everything's going digital. Our advertisers can't afford to support the cost of print. We also lose advertisements to the free giveaway paper. They can make it free because they don't pay contributors. I'm banking we can keep current advertisers and reach even more subscribers by offering both print and online editions."

"Can I still work for you?" The paper provided Daisy's only source of income. It would be hard to justify staying in Franklin without it.

"With everything going online, the video reports you and Jake contribute will be even more important, and, if things work as expected, you'll both get raises."

"Well, that's a huge relief. Thanks for letting me know. I'm off now, ok?"

At the B&P gas station close to her office, she filled up the Jeep and got a Coke. The cold carbonation and caffeine gave her just the boost needed to proceed. She began the long drive back to the crash site and on to the Walkers' place. She had not thought it necessary to tell Chad about that destination, especially since she believed he would nix it, just as Jake had. Daisy was determined to be at the right place at the right time — now or never.

CHAPTER 5

Once Daisy exited the parkway and began the slow climb up Ruby Mine Road, she thought about the Walkers. Caleb Walker had been in her class at school until he dropped out. He was a shy boy. She never made fun of him, but the other kids did because he seemed to wear the same clothes every day and he smelled bad. Once she asked if he had a mother. She could not imagine a mother letting her child go to school in that condition. Daisy never forgot his answer, "She ain't well." Daisy often lent him paper and pencils on the sly after that. She liked him because he made good grades and did not cause any trouble like some of the other boys.

When they went to Franklin High and Daisy joined

the cheerleading squad, she met Caleb's older sister Jasmine, who was the head cheerleader. She was Caleb's direct opposite, as perfect as Caleb seemed to be damaged. Her long black hair, straight without using a flat iron, and high cheekbones spoke of a Cherokee ancestry. Her clothes were always clean and pressed, not to mention in the latest style.

Caleb disappeared after ninth grade and, though she wondered what had happened, she never asked Jasmine. A lot of boys left school because their families needed them to work the farms. From things he had written in class she knew he lived higher up the road from the ruby mine and that his mother was an educated woman who met Caleb's father when she was researching native sites and legends.

Daisy decided to stop at the mine for another Coke with a side of gossip. Louisa Simpson should know more than anyone about what happened on the mountain last night.

The parking lot at Simpson's was half full, typical for late autumn when children were back at school and the retirees had returned from up north to spend fall and winter in the mountains. Louisa was sitting behind the counter. She had sifting screens ready on the shelf behind her, where a sign read, 1 bucket $20, 2 buckets $30, umbrellas with stand $5.

Daisy took her pad and pen out.

"Hi, Daisy," Louisa said. "Taking a day off to play?"

"No, ma'am, working," Daisy said, "What have you heard about the plane crash last night?"

"Not too much. You?"

"Come on. You know I was up there. At the crash site?"

"Well, saw you drive past, didn't I?"

Frustrated, Daisy thought a minute. Louisa Simpson was a heavy-set mountain woman, born on this very mountain. Her long hair, once a glistening black, was now gray and wiry. Nowadays her only activity was sitting behind this counter to collect rent on buckets of earth and screens for the tourists. She also did the cooking and housekeeping. Her husband and sons did the mining. She kept the few raw gems worth anything and salted buckets with the others to keep the tourists at work and coming back.

"Now, Louisa, you know I'm not here to cause you any trouble. It's just my job, to report on incidents like this to the best of my ability; and I need to ask people like you if they have anything to add. OK? I'm not drawing you in deeper into this accident. I just want to know if you know anything that I don't, ok?"

"I know, Daisy," Louisa finally agreed. "This look like a mess anyway you look at it. I don't want to be mixed up in it."

"I understand that. I'll keep your name out of it if you can help. Have you seen anything that I might not have?"

"The NTSB boys are already up there. Some of'em left their cars in the lot."

"That seems fast for a small plane crash!" Daisy said. "I wonder why?"

"Don't know. The fire trucks cleared out by noon; then NTSB arrived. That's all I know."

"Have you seen anyone else on the mountain? Strangers?"

"I dunno. Might've been some kind of Feds, but I mind my own business. Keepin' out of trouble."

"Anything else unusual?"

"Nope. Told you everything I know. Now I gotta get to work."

With that, Louisa picked up her walkie-talkie, "Eric, I need more supplies up here."

"10-4" was the static-blurred reply.

Louisa turned to the wooden shelves behind her and got two screens to put on the counter. Sure enough, a family of four entered the shop, mom and dad with boy and girl too young for school.

"Morning, folks," Louisa greeted them. "Feeling lucky today?"

"You betcha," said the father.

They traded money for gear.

"Come back if you need an umbrella for the sun," Louisa called after them.

Daisy gave it one more try.

"Louisa, I just have two questions, ok?"

Louisa nodded and looked her dead-on in the eye.

"Did you hear or see the plane crash?"

"First, I heard was a plane flying too low. I could tell it was small by the sound and it was close. Then the crash. Over in just a few seconds. I could tell it was up the mountain from us."

"Have you heard from the Walkers? Do you think they would know anything about it?"

Louisa's eyes lit up at this question, as if it were an idea that she had not thought of herself but liked. She shifted her weight on the bar stool she sat upon.

"You know, could be," she offered. "They're odd folk. Been on this mountain longer than my family. Keep to themselves too much if you ask me."

Daisy thought that was a peculiar observation from someone who kept totally to herself and her kin, but she said nothing. She also thought how odd it was to see Louisa smile. She put her notebook and pen away in her bag.

"Thanks, Louisa."

Daisy got an ice-cold Coke from the antique icebox, paid, and went out to continue her drive to see the Walkers. The wind had picked up and clouds gathered to darken the sky. Sudden gusts attempted to shove the Jeep onto the shoulder, so Daisy gripped the steering wheel tightly and fought to keep the vehicle moving forward.

Late afternoon storms were the rule rather than the exception this time of year, and Daisy hoped it would not be a bad one. Even in her 4WD, she had trouble on the dirt and gravel roads in the mountains after rain turned them into muddy messes.

CHAPTER 6

Next stop, the crash site to see the National Transportation Safety Board at work. She checked her phone for texts. One reminder for the school board meeting; nothing from Jake. *Good, he must not have realized I've gone AWOL.*

The crash site was bustling with varied activities. Several blue-jacketed investigators with NTSB, DEA, ATF, and SBI in large letters on their backs were standing near the road. With them were four or five figures in hazmat suits and oxygen masks.

Down the mountainside two men with chainsaws and one with an axe were hard at work. In the short time Daisy had been gone, they had almost cleared a path through the mountain laurel thickets. She walked down carefully until she came to the first of the men. The letters on his jacket read NTSB.

"Why the hazmat suits?" Daisy asked. "Daisy McLaren, *Franklin Free Press*."

The National Transportation Safety Board representative turned to study her. She showed him her press badge, put it back in her bag and took out her notepad and pen.

"They're testing for air quality before we go farther down," he said. "Standard procedure." His badge identified him as George Altman.

"So, you think there could be dangerous fumes? From drugs? Chemicals?"

"I understand you have a job to do, ma'am, but we don't have any information for you now. You'll have to wait to hear our findings when our report is released."

"But Mr. Altman," Daisy said. "People in town are already guessing. They think it's probably bootleggers bringing liquor or cigarettes to avoid state taxes. But they're also afraid it might be terrorists. Can you at least rule some things out?"

"I'm sorry but that's all for now. This area is restricted."

He called to one of his team. "Please see the lady back to her car and set up a cordon again at the edge of the road."

Daisy knew better than to push back against federal officials, so she let herself be guided to her car.

It could be bootleggers. She and Jake had stumbled across the ruins of a still on one of their hikes. Some people still made their own mash, but most bootleggers smuggled in liquor, as well as cigarettes to avoid high North Carolina taxes.

Daisy made a few notes about what she had seen at the crash site and drove on to visit the Walkers.

CHAPTER 7

The dogs started to bark before Daisy reached the top of the road near the Walker place. She stopped and put the Jeep's windows up. For safe measure, she locked all the doors. Checking her cell again, she saw she had no reception. She thought briefly about going back to get Jake to come with her, but, shaking her head at that idea, she downshifted for the last steep segment of her journey.

She hoped they could provide more information than she had gotten from Louisa Simpson and the NTSB boss. Louisa had claimed ignorance. George Altman had simply said that they would make NTSB findings public when the investigations concluded, and they reviewed the report.

Daisy was angry about being brushed off, but she remembered the advice her father had tried to drum in her head since she was little, *you can catch more flies with honey than vinegar*. She could hear his voice saying the words and knew for sure that he would remind her of that tonight. She knew he wanted to rein Daisy in, to keep her safe. He long tried to imbue her with caution until at last he conceded defeat. *He's afraid I'm too much like mama to change.*

The barking was louder now. Daisy stopped the car. She knew from the sound that these were big dogs, more than one. Digging her phone out of her bag, she tried to text Jake to let him know where she was. Perhaps he would try to stop her again, and this time she would listen. At the very least someone would know where she was. *Still no cell phone service. I might have known. This just isn't my day; but nothing ventured, nothing gained.* The latter had never been advice given to her by Lucas McLaren.

She put the Jeep in first and the back wheels spun in the damp gravel before jerking forward. Within seconds she was in the Walkers' dirt yard. Three well-fed German shepherds jumped and barked at her simultaneously from all sides. Shaking, she lay on her horn, hoping someone would come to her rescue. The cacophony stopped suddenly.

Daisy rested her head on the steering wheel. When she looked up, she saw ahead to the right a single-wide mobile home in a thicket of grass and briars. To her left was a path worn through tall grass and shrubs, where she got a glimpse of another structure and several rusted-out vehicles.

"What are you doing?"

The question startled Daisy. She had to look a little behind her to the right to see where it came from. The still-alert pack of dogs sat on the porch of an ancient log cabin beside an unshaven man in jeans and a T-shirt, cradling a gun across his chest. She regarded him with disbelief because he appeared as such a caricature of a mountain man. Daisy had lived almost all her life in Franklin and had never seen a person who fit the stereotype so well.

Daisy said, "I'm Daisy McLaren with the *Franklin Free Press*. Can I ask you some questions about the plane crash last night?"

"No, you can't," the man said, "and you've got five seconds to get off my property."

"Are you Mr. Walker?"

The man fired a warning shot into the air.

Daisy was bewildered, but he did not have to warn her twice. She began to back up but soon realized that she would have to turn around to make it down the mountain. She spun to the left, backed up and completed the y- turn into the rutted gravel and dirt road. At that moment, the heavens opened with a crack of thunder, and the rains came down like the waterfalls in the Cullasaja Gap.

CHAPTER 8

Jake had tried to warn her off going to see the Walkers by herself, and Daisy now wished she had the sense to listen for once. She had figured the Walkers would be eccentric and not forthcoming, but she had not expected that they would be violent. She had not been prepared to be threatened with a gun; however, she still wanted to find out what they might know about the plane crash, and right now she felt they were her best bet for information. She decided not to tell Jake about her unsuccessful first attempt to interview them.

A flash of lightning and a crack of thunder brought Daisy back from her thoughts. The heavy rain blurred the view ahead. She set the wipers to the highest speed.

The rapid movement of the wipers annoyed her. That they improved her ability to see the road not at all annoyed her more.

Daisy knew she should pull over until the onslaught of rain lessened. Had she been on the interstate she would have done that, pulled over with her flashers on. Here she was determined at least to get to a spot where she would have a good cell phone reception, so she forged ahead.

Daisy tried to steer the Jeep away from the road's edge, but hitting a deep rut in the road, she overcorrected. The Jeep bounced off the rocky face of the cliff that loomed above her. Daisy managed to get control again, but fast-moving water gushing down the road grabbed hold of the four-wheel-drive vehicle and carried it down until it crashed into an ancient boulder.

Not that it mattered as she had no reception, but her cell phone's battery was dying. "What else can go wrong?" Daisy wondered aloud. She put on her windbreaker and attempted to get out to walk to a better area, but the steady stream of fast-moving water caught her legs, throwing her off balance. She held tight to the door, caught hold of the steering wheel and pulled herself back into the Jeep.

Daisy's heart was pounding, and she had to fight to catch breath. Her anxiety was mounting, and she began to hyperventilate. Afraid of fainting, she made a conscious effort to breathe slowly and deeply until she regained control. All she needed was to have a panic attack while stranded on the mountainside.

The rain had stopped, but the woods were so dark that Daisy suspected another downpour could come at any moment. She snatched a sweater from the back seat. Nights were cold in this late autumn, and she was not yet used to them after a hot and dry Indian summer that seemed to linger forever. Her clothes were soaked through, and she shivered in the night. She held the sweater up close to her chin and stretched it over her shoulders. She breathed into her hands, which grasped the wool and felt some welcomed warmth.

Soaking wet and out of breath, she closed her eyes to rest. As she fell asleep, she saw a dim light flashing in the distance.

CHAPTER 9

A faint light glowed in the gray misty woods. It swayed back and forth as it moved up the mountain. Daisy rubbed her sleep-filled eyes to sharpen her focus. Men on horseback followed by pack donkeys and men walking. Lanterns held high ahead of the cavalry and foot soldiers as they made their way through the ivy. Daisy was certain she was seeing a phantom army attempting to cross over the ridge. Last to come was a soldier leading a team of dray horses, which pulled a small cannon mounted on a cart.

Daisy looked again at the ghostly procession. Close to the front was a standard bearer. The red on white Burgundy Cross announced that this was a medieval army of Spain. Right behind was a soldier in armor accompanied by a native maiden. It must be de Soto with the Indian princess, Daisy thought again. Their muscular horses were so close she could touch them.

She debated about getting out to inspect the phantom army. Against even her own better judgement, she was putting on her rain boots to do just that when she heard a noise. Turning to look, the appearance of the face of a Cherokee warrior startled her, in red and black war paint, up close to the window beside her. He shook his war club made of wood, leather and deer antler honed to a sharp edge at her, and then with a warrior's cry he disappeared into the thicket. Daisy heard the laurel and rhododendron branches rustling and assumed that many natives must be following the warrior she had seen. Cherokee braves making sure their princess was safe.

Finally, the thicket was still and dark. The rain pounded her jeep again. Daisy slept to its steady music.

CHAPTER 10

An insistent rapping gradually grew louder until it startled Daisy awake. "Are they gone?" she exclaimed.

"I reckon. Who are we talking about?" A tall figure covered with a slick black rain poncho stood in the still heavy rain beside her car. He leaned close into the window.

"The natives," she began, until she realized she was talking to Jake, who was grinning at her.

Jake laughed. "Just you, me, and some bears up here, darlin'. Let's get you out of here to some place warm and dry."

CHAPTER

11

Wrapped in a soft blanket Jake had brought along specially for her, Daisy rested. Her head leaned against the window. Jake had turned the radio on low. Willie was singing "To All the Girls I've Loved Before" and Jake hummed along.

When the truck hit the pavement at the end of the gravel road, Daisy's head hit the window and she sat up with a jerk. It took her a minute to realize where she was and what had happened. She knew she had only dreamed of Hernando de Soto and the Cherokee princess, but Daisy was certain she had seen a light through the storm on the mountain. It was a faint white light moving steadily, but rather than moving toward the top of the ridge, it descended toward the valley. Someone moving in a cabin in the woods or headlights on a car? If she were still up there, could she find out?

Daisy leaned her head back against the window and glared at Jake. "Who asked for your help? I was just waiting for the storm to ease up."

"Well, excuse me for helping," Jake replied. "Just say the word and I'll take you right back up there." Daisy turned her head away.

Jake continued, "So you were planning to walk for help? Guess you haven't heard we're getting a tropical storm from the remnants of a hurricane out of the Gulf."

A Category 4 hurricane had been pounding the Alabama-Mississippi border before heading north. Daisy knew it had aimed at Franklin, but she had not planned on getting caught in it.

"It's stalled over us," Jake said, "so you can expect this weather for the next few days."

No reply.

"Well, if that's the way you want to play it," Jake laughed as he turned the radio back on. Ronnie Milsap was singing "Smoky Mountain Rain." Jake sang along.

Even in his 2012 Dodge Ram 1500, Jake took it slow in the tropical storm. The rain made a steady wet sheet on his windshield despite the wiper action. Forward vision was nonexistent, so Jake felt his way down the ancient road.

"I've driven these roads thousands of times over the years," he suddenly told Daisy. "There's this one spot where I'd park and hike up or down into the woods to hunt for deer and wild turkey. I'd tromp through the thickets of laurel and brambles until I reached my deer stand in a white oak about a mile up the mountain where once I shot a bear. That was the only bear I ever killed."

Jake paused and looked at Daisy.

"I remember," Daisy murmured. "That was summer after senior year."

"I was up high in the oak and the bear had not seen me. I could have only watched and let the gigantic old male amble on down the mountain to forage, but I fired and killed him with one shot from my old Remington. "

"I gave the bearskin to the man who cut up, packaged and froze the meat and handed out brown paper grocery bags full of frozen bear meat to my teachers, my friends' families, the preacher," he continued. "Still, it seemed I ate bear meat in some form all winter, bear stew, bear steaks, bear chili. Chili, if very spicy, was sometimes good, but mainly the meat tasted as if the bear had been scavenging in dumpsters and on carrion before heading to its den to hibernate."

"It might have been that my feeling guilty made it taste so awful."

"No," Daisy laughed, "you gave us a lot of chili, and it was terrible." She stuck out her tongue and winced at the memory of the taste.

Daisy leaned against Jake's shoulder and feigned sleep until they got to the driveway she shared with her father. Jake turned off the engine. Daisy remained still and quiet. The warmth of his body continued to calm her, and she was hesitant to give that up.

Jake reached his left hand over and gently jostled her. "Daisy? Can you wake up? You're home."

She sat up slowly and hugged the blanket closer around her. Her thoughts were as tangled as the laurel branches twisting and stretching to find sunlight. Abruptly she opened the cab's door and leapt out.

Daisy said, "Don't bother coming in," she said. "I know you think I need rescuing and don't know how to handle myself, but I don't."

With that, she slammed it shut and stormed up the stairs to her apartment.

She heard him say, "Back to normal, I guess," as he parked his truck and knocked on Lucas McLaren's door.

CHAPTER 12

Daisy was up at dawn the next morning. Looking out the window, she saw the wind blowing the rain hard and sideways. Leaves and tree branches littered the yard.

Her room was a mess; she was without her Jeep; and, to make matters worse, the internet was out. Stiffer than usual after the previous night's ordeal, she stayed longer in her hot shower before dressing. Considering her options, she used the time straightening and cleaning.

She sorted her clothes into two laundry bags, one for the dry cleaners and one to wash. Her lingerie was already soaking in the bathroom sink. She worked methodically through the apartment, loading the dishwasher, wiping down countertops, swiffering, and vacuuming floors. Satisfied all was thoroughly clean, she made a cup of Maxwell House in her Keurig and sat down to watch the morning news.

At least one more day of a tropical storm was predicted. Trees were down. Crewmen were working to restore power to the entire county. Internet service was out across all providers. The worst effects of the storm had been on the mountainsides, with two rockslides, one that had closed the highway between Franklin and Sylva, the principal route to both Asheville and Cherokee.

Daisy put on her slicker and rain boots, grabbed the laundry bag and a set of keys to the main house. The storm was still strong. As she struggled to pull the door closed, a small wet figure dashed inside. When it sat down facing her, she saw it was a small and scrawny cat. With rain gear already wet, she put off dealing with it until after she got her laundry started. She didn't bother to lock the door behind her but leaned into the storm to fight her way down the steps. The hood blew off her head and, by the time she got to her father's porch, she was soaked head to shoulders.

When Lucas's forefathers built a new house in 1852, they constructed a two-story house with a central hall, like the dogtrot log cabin of the first McLarens to settle in Franklin, with shed roof porches on front and back.

The kitchen in the new house had been in a separate building to contain fires. Lucas had placed the current kitchen on that same site and had kept the large stone fireplace and hearth. Many of the former tools and gadgets for open hearth cooking remained, large andirons to hold the logs, a hook to swing large pots over the fire.

Daisy unlocked the door and entered the large warm kitchen.

No lights were on. She got her early bird nature from her mother. Lucas McLaren had never been an early riser. She dropped the bags by the door and turned on the overhead light. Lucas was as organized and tidy as Daisy was messy and chaotic. Coffee had been set up the night before, so she just flipped the switch and waited. There were two mugs on the counter. One was Carolina Blue. He had calculated she would be over.

"I don't know how he does that," she said out loud. She pressed the button to stop the brewing and poured herself a cup. Carrying it to the kitchen table, she switched on the wall-mounted television already tuned to WLOS.

"News 13 has just learned that an additional mudslide has blocked the highway between Highlands and Franklin," the long-time anchorman said. "Crews are on the way to evaluate the damage, and of course WLOS will be there too and will keep you posted throughout the day about developments.

"On the bright side, we have an update on the weather. The storm is moving and should be out of here by suppertime. For more on that, here's Laura Tomkins. Over to you, Laura. What can you tell us?"

"Well, Chris, a picture says a thousand words, so let's look at the map. I'm removing some color so we can see the different issues...."

Daisy turned off the TV. She had heard enough. She hoped storm interference with the huge satellite receiver on a nearby mountaintop had caused the interruption in internet service. If power could be restored by evening, she could complete her vlog and post the stories online from her laptop.

Like most rural newspapers, the *Free Press* had developed a sophisticated website to provide current information. Daisy posted her vlog *Macon County: History & Legend* there every Friday evening. She had developed a large following that extended to Highlands, Hayesville, and towns in the Georgia foothills.

Lucas McLaren came into the kitchen using his walker, as his daughter was pouring cornflakes into a bowl.

"I'm making waffles," he said.

In his threadbare robe loosely tied over pajamas that clearly had a lot of mileage on them, he resembled a retiree instead of the top lawyer in Western North Carolina that he was.

"No need. I'm sticking with cereal. And coffee, of course. Here's a cup for you."

Lucas scratched his head and followed his daughter to the kitchen table.

"No paper?" he mumbled.

"I didn't look."

Lucas took the glasses off the top of his head and smoothed his hair.

"Daddy, I need to use your car today. OK?"

Before Lucas could answer, they heard a toilet being flushed. Daisy looked toward the hall and then at her father. She heard someone coming down the stairs.

"Daddy?"

"Well, I couldn't send him back out in the storm when he'd just saved your life. Could I?"

Wearing another ratty-looking robe, Jake entered the kitchen to catch the tail end of the talk. He could imagine how Daisy would respond to that assertion.

"Saved my life? Really? I was doing just fine."

Jake knew better than to argue with Daisy. It would be a long, hard day if he started off with a debate. He ignored the discussion.

"Any more coffee?"

"Get your own. Where's your truck anyhow?"

"Garage."

"OK. I'm going to get ready for work and you can take me to town. Thirty minutes. Daddy, can you please check on the Jeep?"

The two men nodded. Daisy put her laundry in the washer and left the house.

"That's my girl," Lucas said what Jake was thinking.

CHAPTER 13

Daisy struggled against the rain and wind to return to her apartment. Once up the exterior stairs, she yanked the wood door open against the wind and rain. The gale-force winds blew her into the living room and slammed the door shut behind her.

As she turned to go to her bedroom, she saw a small black, white, and orange cat preening herself on the small kitchen table. It barely glanced at her.

"Dang!" she said. "I'd forgotten about you."

The little calico ignored Daisy and continued to lick her paw and rub it past her ears and down her brow.

"Hmph," Daisy said, "I'll take care of you on my way out."

Daisy showered and dressed in record time. She figured correctly that it would be a waste of time in this weather to dry her hair and put on make-up. After donning her slicker and pulling on her rain boots, she returned to the great room to put the cat out, but there was no cat to be seen. She looked under the table and couch. The room was not so big that there could be loads of hiding places.

Thinking the stray might have slipped past her, Daisy returned to her bedroom. Not there. She even called out, "Here kitty. Come here, cat."

I don't have time for this.

Daisy took the time to fill a shallow bowl with water and set it by the kitchen counter. Believing that she had more important things to do today, she decided she could deal with the cat problem later and pushed her way outside once more.

She walked into Lucas's kitchen for the second time that morning while Lucas was still in his old bathrobe. Before joining him at the table, she draped the slicker over a chair and poured herself another cup of coffee.

"I can use your help, Dad."

"What do you need?"

Daisy stirred her coffee.

"I'm working on a new story for my vlog about Franklin." She paused and looked Lucas in the eye. "What do you know about de Soto and the Cherokee princess?"

Lucas laughed.

"Is that all? You looked so anxious about asking me I thought you might want to ask about one of my clients, and you know I can't discuss details about them with anyone."

Daisy thought for a moment about the car crash that took her mother's life when Daisy was about to graduate from the university in Chapel Hill. That was the question Daisy always wanted to bring up because she thought Lucas still held back certain details about the crash, thinking that she was not strong enough to hear them. She loved how protective of her Lucas was, even as she struggled to be independent.

Lucas took a sip of coffee as Jake entered the room, coat on, keys in hand.

"Alright, let's get this show on the road."

"In a minute. I've got to talk to Dad first."

"And I've got to be at work ten minutes ago. If you want a ride with me, in the truck."

Lucas intervened.

"Go on. I can tell you what I remember this evening."

"Promise?" Daisy asked.

Lucas nodded. He was about to ask her why she seemed so worried about it. Before he could, Daisy spoke.

"You'll check on my car?"

"Of course, sweetie. Now go on. Come to my office around four, and we can ride home together."

Daisy nodded her head, put on her raincoat, and picked up her laptop. Jake held the door open, and, after saluting Lucas McLaren, darted out after her to his Dodge truck.

"The *Free Press*?" Jake asked.

"No," Daisy said. "Take me to the sheriff's office. I've got to check on something."

Jake drove the truck carefully through the town. They had to take a detour where a tree had fallen knocking down power lines. As they started up the hill toward downtown Franklin, Daisy gathered her things. She knew that she ought to thank Jake for coming out in the storm to search for her, but she had a hard time settling on what to say.

"Thank you for not saying I told you so," she finally said, "and I guess I should thank you for going out in the storm to check on me. And for taking me home."

Daisy rarely admitted she needed help, that she might ever be vulnerable. Jake glanced at Daisy.

"Darlin', it was my pleasure," he chortled as he spoke.

Daisy drew back and raised her eyebrows in disbelief. Things were back to normal.

Jake pulled his Dodge Ram into a space in front of the sheriff's office.

"The paper wants some photos and a story about the storm damage online by dinnertime. Why don't I pick you up for lunch and we can ride around and get that done?"

Daisy thought for a minute. She wanted to go to the Macon County Historical Museum after meeting with Ben Williams. "You're going to have to handle that all by your lonesome, okay? I have to see what I can find out about de Soto, or Chad will have my head, not to mention my job."

With that, Daisy jumped out of Jake's truck saying, "I can write the copy when I get back to the office." Then she darted into the county building. Her top priority was finding out if there was any new information about the plane crash and especially whether anyone else had spotted the man running away from the area. If no one could connect him with the crash, perhaps someone had seen a new person in town, one who did not seem entirely comfortable, who might look as though he were trying unsuccessfully to be inconspicuous.

Once she had learned all she could from the sheriff, she would return to work on the article about de Soto in Franklin. Her vision or dream on the mountain had unsettled her and had awakened her curiosity in the old legend. She now thought there might be something to it and the Museum seemed the best place to start her investigation in earnest.

CHAPTER 14

The sheriff was not in his office when Daisy arrived. There were several deputies clustered around the coffeemaker. They nodded at Daisy as she passed by. She had known all of them most of her life, but she did not stop to chat. Instead, she headed into Maxie's office.

Maxie was the administrator, dispatcher, and mom to the men and one woman in the department. She had been at the job long before Williams was elected. Daisy remembered seeing her at this same desk as a child when she would come with her dad to pick up clients. Maxie was auburn-haired, blue-eyed, simply dressed, with an ample bosom on which the teens of Franklin could cry before being taken to the cells to sober up after a night of underage drinking. Many Friday nights she worked late to be there for them when they had celebrated a win or loss at the football game.

Since her husband passed away two years ago after a twenty-two-year marriage, many men in the area had asked her out, hoping to be the one to replace her Tom. Thus far Maxie had stuck to work, church, and home. She did not seem to be ready for any next stage of life.

"Hey, Maxie, have you heard much about the plane crash the other night?"

"Hi there, Daisy! You probably know more than I do. Ben said you were up there, too. The only thing I could tell you is that we've been busy, and the phone has been ringing off the hook."

"I just know there was more to it than just an accident, and now I'm positive the Walkers are involved," Daisy said. "Swear to keep a secret?"

"I don't know about that."

Daisy pleaded with her eyes. "Maxie?"

"Since it's you, I swear."

Daisy recounted her visit to the Walkers' property and ended with, "Then he fired his shotgun."

"At you?"

Daisy shook her head. "In the air. But I think he would've shot at me if I hadn't got out there fast."

Maxie stood up, walked over, and took Daisy by both shoulders. "Ben really should know about this."

"Maxie, you swore."

"And I'll keep my word, if you promise to tell Ben before the end of the day."

"I promise. I know you're right. I just need to put all the pieces together in my mind."

At that moment Sheriff Williams walked in accompanied by a rather tall man in a dark suit, white shirt, and striped tie.

The sheriff nodded at Daisy and said to Maxie, "I'll be tied up for an hour. Hold my calls."

"Can I still interview you this afternoon?" Daisy said.

"Sure thing, Daisy. Come back around 2:30."

The men went into Ben's office, and Ben closed the door behind them.

"Who is that?" Daisy asked.

"Someone important, that's for sure," Maxie said. "There have been a lot of people come here from Atlanta and Asheville, and he's the only one Ben's brought to the office."

"Can I call you later to find out?"

"Maybe Ben will tell you when you talk to him later."

"Right," Daisy said, already trying to figure out how to avoid telling Ben that Walker had threatened her with his shotgun until she had figured out how the Walkers were involved in the plane crash. Jake and her father would be on her case hard enough without the sheriff joining in too. She needed to have freedom of movement to get to the bottom of this incident.

Daisy weighed her possibilities for the day. She realized that she would need a car to accomplish everything she had to do. She decided to walk over to Stamey's Café for lunch. Stamey's was always a good place for local gossip as well. She could work on her story and then either walk or get a ride uphill to her father's law office.

She was finishing the grilled cheese sandwich and Coke that she always ordered at Stamey's and was about to pack up her work when Sheriff Williams walked in with the stranger. To her surprise they stopped at her table.

"Daisy," the sheriff said, "mind if we join you?"

"Course not," she said. "I'm about to leave but have a seat."

"This is Nathan Stark. He'll be supervising the operations at the plane crash so you can bug him for info." Ben chuckled as he said this. "He's with the FBI in Atlanta, but I'd like his presence here to be off the record for now."

"Nathan, this is Miss Daisy McLaren, Franklin's star reporter."

If Daisy could have kicked his shin under the table, she would have. Instead, she said, "I always told the sheriff that I wouldn't have to bug him if he'd just take me along on his calls."

The ice was broken.

"I'll remember that," Nathan said.

"I tell you what, I won't spill the beans about your being here to investigate the plane crash, if you promise to sit down and give me an exclusive interview when you're done. Deal?"

"Deal!"

They shook on it and Daisy made a quick escape before the sheriff could embarrass her again.

Despite her embarrassment, she had been able to check out the change in Nathan Stark's appearance. He had shed the suit for khaki slacks and a dark blue polo shirt that showed off his build. Quite different from the guys she had hung out with in Chapel Hill. Nathan appeared to be someone who worked out and trained every day to be ready for any situation he might face on the job.

Daisy could not help comparing him to Jake whose sinewy strength came from working long hours on his mother's farm. He had kept it going since his father disappeared when they were in high school. The farm was much smaller than it had been. Jake grew no cash crops and instead focused on maintaining a garden patch what produced vegetables year-round. Chickens, a small herd of goats, and a cow completed the enterprise. Jake made a little extra money by leasing out the goat herd to clear pastures and lawns that were overgrown and seldom used.

CHAPTER 15

Hey, Maxie," Daisy said, "is the sheriff back?"

Maxie stopped typing, took out her earphones, and looked up. The office was old school and Ben Williams preferred to use a Dictaphone for reports. He had never learned to type, and Maxie had never learned shorthand. They had both been sent for technology training in Asheville but, as they worked on a need-to-know basis, the training did not take. So Ben used the recorder and Maxie either typed directly into forms on her old typewriter or typed longer summaries into a basic Word document.

"Not yet, but Jake's already here. He's in Ben's office."

"Thanks." Daisy went down the hall and turned

into Ben's office where Jake was setting up the equipment he used for indoor recording. He had affixed the camera to a tripod facing a large wall map of Macon County. "Hi, Jake."

"Hello there, darlin'," he said. "I was thinking you could use the map to talk about what happened the other morning. Here's your mic." He motioned her over and reached to attach the Bluetooth microphone to her shirt.

Daisy took it from his hand. "I can manage that." She clipped it to her shirt and walked over to study the map just as Ben walked in.

He gave Daisy a quick hug and shook hands with Jake. "I'm ready if you are." He knew the drill and took a second microphone from Jake. Attaching it to his collar, he took his place beside Daisy at the map.

"Where's Nathan?" Daisy said. "I thought we might include him in the interview."

"Had another meeting. Y'all ready?"

Jake nodded his head at Daisy, who looked directly at the camera where a red light was flashing.

"I'm here with Sheriff Ben Williams to learn more about the small plane crash that startled the mountain town of Franklin Wednesday night." She turned to Ben. "Mr. Williams..."

"Daisy," Jake interrupted, "call him Sheriff Williams or Ben. We're not in high school anymore."

She glared at Jake and turned to the sheriff.

"I'm here with Sheriff Ben Williams to learn more about the small plane crash that startled the mountain town of Franklin Wednesday night. Sheriff Williams, I understand you have received the findings of the National Transportation Safety Board."

"That's right." Ben held up a folder.

"Can you share them with us?"

Ben took out a single page. "I'll summarize it for you. A combination of pilot error and poor visibility in the tropical storm caused the crash. The Cessna was registered in Atlanta, and the pilot was not the registered owner. There was no flight plan filed."

"Do you have any more information about the pilot?"

"We're waiting for the results of the autopsy from Raleigh. We're withholding the name until we can confirm his identity."

Daisy motioned toward the map. "Can you show us where the crash happened?"

"The crash site was located about a mile past the Simpson's ruby mine." He pointed to the area. "It was approximately 100 yards downhill from the road."

"That's the length of a football field. Right, sheriff?"

"That's correct, Daisy. And the ivy thickets made the recovery of the body and the investigation extremely difficult."

"What do you know about the other man, running downhill into the forest away from the crash?"

"There was only the dead pilot at the site of the crash." Daisy let this drop for now.

"Is there anything you'd like to add?"

Sheriff Williams looked directly at the camera. "I'd

like to ask members of the public to contact me if you have any knowledge about this plane or the pilot. You can also call our tip line to leave an anonymous message."

"Thank you, Sheriff Williams. This is Daisy McLaren reporting from Franklin, North Carolina, for WLOS news, and be sure to follow me on Twitter, Facebook, and Instagram for the latest in Macon County news."

Daisy relaxed. She removed the microphone, walked over, and returned it to Jake who was already dismantling the tripod and packing up.

"I'll send a copy to WLOS. I'll send you a copy for your vlog once I've edited the last bit to remove WLOS."

"Thanks." Daisy gathered her things and left the office. Down the hall she stopped again to chat with Maxie. Maxie had had her hair done and was dressed simply in black slacks, a crisp white shirt, ruby earrings, and a large ruby pendant. She looked stunning as usual.

"Hey, Maxie," Daisy said, "isn't that the ruby your dad found when you were a little girl?"

"Yes! It's the family treasure. Daddy found it in a stream on our land and actually carried it over to Asheville for a jeweler there to cut it and set it. Mama only wore it on their anniversary and her birthday. She gave it to me before she passed."

"It's so beautiful! You must be going someplace special tonight?"

Maxie blushed and touched the pendant.

"Not really, but Friday there's a new James Bond

movie at the Ruby Cinema. You going?"

"I guess. I haven't really thought about it. Special date?"

Ruby smiled mysteriously. "You'll see if you're there."

Certain that Maxie was keeping something or someone a secret, Daisy thought about prying for more information but thought better and decided to wait. She could always ask Ben about it.

"Well, I guess I'd better be there. I think I can talk Jake into going to see a Bond movie. Where did Jake disappear to?"

Jake had gone without saying goodbye.

"Speaking of Jake," Maxie said, "what's going on with you two? Are you dating again?'

"Me and Jake? Are you kidding?" Daisy rolled her eyes and brushed her hair behind her ear with her right hand. "Been there, done that! We've been good friends forever!"

"That doesn't mean that you can't have a relationship now. It seems y'all are always together."

Daisy shook her head vigorously. "Don't try to start any rumors, Maxie. Save your counseling for the teenagers at Franklin High. For my part, I'm focusing on my career and moving onward and upward. I plan to be in Raleigh or Charlotte before I'm thirty."

CHAPTER 16

When Daisy entered his law office, Lucas McLaren was sitting in a leather armchair and reading the *Atlanta Constitution-Journal*. He had been in court earlier in the day for two Franklin teenagers caught with a brick of marijuana and charged with possession with intent to distribute. The boys came from one of Franklin's finest families.

After calling many character witnesses including the pastor of the Methodist Church, Lucas convinced the judge that the youths simply had too much time and money and that they had no need or intention of selling. They left the court owing a $1000 fine and 60 hours of community service. The judge also recommended that the parents limit the amount of money given in allowance and help their children find after-school work, paid or volunteer once their community service was completed.

The other case he took to court involved pro bono work for a nineteen-year-old construction worker who had been found asleep and drunk in his pickup truck stopped on the side of the road. He had been working construction since he was seventeen and already had a wife and child. Lucas was able to get limited driving privileges for him to drive to and from work and for work activities.

Lucas closed the newspaper, folded it, and set it on the table. He looked over his glasses at his daughter.

"Bad news, your car's totaled."

Daisy groaned.

"Good news, I could get you a new Jeep that should be ready in the morning."

"Thank you."

Lucas motioned to the matching leather sofa.

"We've got some time here. Let's sit and talk a while."

"Tell me. Why are you so interested in what I know about de Soto and the Indian maiden? I know you're researching for your vlog, but why were you so anxious about asking? That's not like you."

Daisy glanced away. Then back at Lucas.

"When I was on the mountain—after the crash, I saw them. I mean, I thought I saw them. First, I saw a lantern light followed by de Soto and the maiden with Spanish soldiers. Then a Cherokee warrior banged on the car window with his tomahawk. I thought he was going to kill me."

Daisy shivered and crossed her arms. Lucas sat back in his armchair.

"Sweetheart," he said gently, "you were probably in shock from the accident. You've had the legend on your mind, so no wonder you dreamed, or imagined, that. You know it couldn't really have happened, don't you?"

"I know, but it seemed like it was really there."

Lucas raised his eyebrows.

"Even if I dreamed all that about de Soto, I know I saw a light moving in the woods."

Lucas laughed.

"I'll grant you that, and I'm sure there is a good explanation for it. As for the rest, I don't know much about the actual legend. When I was a boy, the grownups used to tell us ghost stories about the Spaniards, de Soto, as well as the Cherokee. Most of them were blood-chilling. They told us those stories to frighten us and to keep us out of the forest, where real dangers lurked. Black bear, snakes, among others. It worked."

"I didn't go out by myself until I was old enough to hunt, and I rarely went out alone even then. Most of what I could tell you about that legend is in books."

He chuckled.

"The made-up part was that the ghosts of the Spanish soldiers killed at the Nikwasi mound haunt the woods, looking for and killing any descendants of the Cherokee who slaughtered them; that ghosts of Cherokee braves, who had sworn to kill the Spanish and anyone who interferes with their raids, lurked in the forests."

"And you fell for that!" Daisy laughed.

"Well look, I was only eight or nine. I was still having nightmares, and I had a big imagination, too. Like I told you, it worked. I didn't go in the forest alone until I was in high school and went hunting. The only times I went before then were with my father or with the Boy Scouts."

Lucas picked up a small blue book from his table and handed it to Daisy. "I think you'll find all you need to know in this."

"*Cherokee Indian Lore & Smoky Mountain Stories* by Margaret R. Siler," Daisy said. "Thanks, Daddy. I was going to look for a copy."

"Satisfied?"

In answer, Daisy hugged him.

"Let's go home."

Lucas grabbed the walker leaning against the side of his desk and pushed the two buttons to unfold it. He put his briefcase in the attached basket. Bracing himself on the walker, he stood and took a step forward.

"I'm good to go," he said and then shouted to Maxie, "See you tomorrow."

Daisy and Lucas exited through the rear door of the office building. When Lucas first showed signs of Post-Polio Syndrome, they had constructed a gently sloping covered ramp to the parking lot where Lucas had a reserved parking space. For a while he had relied on handrails to brace himself when climbing stairs, but Daisy kept needling him until he had the ramp constructed. She held her umbrella over his head as he got in the car.

The cloudy sky had brightened as the day went on but in the last hour had turned charcoal gray and the winds whipped against the trees. The windshield wipers swished mercilessly back and forth in an attempt to clear the sheets of rain blanketing the glass, but their effort was in vain.

Ultimately Daisy slowed the car to a snail's pace and turned on her emergency flashers so others could see the car as it inched along the route. She was thankful her work was over for the day, and she was grateful to have Lucas in the car with her. His presence always made her feel protected and safe.

Stoplights hung on wires across the intersections swayed wildly as Daisy drove through the small town on the way home.

Nature was allowing the tropical storm to have the last word on this day.

CHAPTER 17

Daisy and Lucas were late getting to the house so, instead of going to her apartment, she stayed for supper with Lucas and Ed.

Ed had been a sergeant in the army and had served two full tours in Afghanistan. He received an honorable discharge in the middle of his third tour and was sent to Walter Reed with a diagnosis of Post-Traumatic Stress Disorder with panic attacks. Months of cognitive therapy and medication provided relief from the worst symptoms, but he relied primarily on exercise to keep his PTSD under control. He had returned home to Franklin.

Now Ed worked days at the Franklin Health & Fitness Center. He had arranged with the owners for veterans to receive free memberships and he organized exercise boot camps specifically for them.

Nights he came to cook for Lucas and assist him as needed. After supper he retired to a bedroom upstairs where he watched TV until time to help Lucas get ready for bed. Three days a week he helped Lucas with physical therapy before work.

The arrangement suited them all. In Daisy's opinion, Ed was a better cook than either Daisy or Lucas. This evening he fed them chicken cordon bleu with broccoli and mashed potatoes. He had seasoned the potatoes with pepper and garlic salt. This was Daisy's favorite meal.

With Ed at the house, Daisy did not worry so much about her father. She suspected Lucas did not actually need for Ed to stay over, but that he was trying to show her she need not stay in Franklin on his account. It was not working. Ed had been with them for over two years, yet still Daisy remained at home. Her latest excuse was that she needed to become better known in order to get a good job in Raleigh or Charlotte. The reality was with her degree in Media and Journalism combined with a portfolio of work done at UNC, she could get an entry-level position with any newspaper or television station in the state, but until she came to terms with the accident that took her mother's life, she was stuck.

Daisy took up the plates when they had finished eating and carried them to the sink to rinse them and load the dishwasher.

"Hey, Ed," Daisy said, "you heard anything about

the plane crash?"

"Not really," he replied. "Do you want some help with those?"

"No, thanks."

"I tell you what you ought to look into once you're done with the crash—the new heroin that's in town. There's oxycontin too, but the heroin right now is cheaper. I think they're trying to get people hooked."

"Why? What's happened?"

"Some kids were messing with it down by the lake, and one almost overdosed. I was at the hospital seeing a patient when they brought him in. If they hadn't had a cellphone with them to call emergency, he would have died for sure."

"Who was it?"

"Joe Taylor."

"You're kidding?"

The Taylors lived down the street from Lucas, and Daisy babysat for Joe when she was in high school. She remembered him as a scrawny kid. Scrawny but cute. Black hair and dark eyes, a reflection of his Cherokee lineage. She recalled when he lost his first tooth, put it under his pillow for the tooth fairy, and later told her he only got "one thin dime."

His family had owned the only bookstore in town, a store that specialized in used books and catered to the tourists who came year-round for different reasons. The locals bought their books at Walmart or online from Amazon. They sold the store when Daisy was away at college, but Joe still worked there after school and during summer vacation. Daisy had never seen him with the fast crowd hanging noisily out at Sonic or at the downtown parks.

"But he's always been such a good kid," Daisy moaned. "How does that even happen?"

Lucas now entered the conversation. "You shouldn't be so surprised, Daisy."

Daisy joined them at the table. Lucas continued, "You know there's still nothing for young people to do here. When you were a teen, other kids got together to drink beer or grain alcohol. I was lucky with you."

Daisy thought about the time she and Jake had tried moonshine on one of their mountain hikes. It did not take much of that liquor for them to get drunk. They had to stay longer than usual to sober up enough to make it back to Jake's truck without falling into a ravine.

"Your mother made sure you were kept busy. She encouraged you to sign up to work on the school paper and yearbook. Kept you at church almost all day on Sunday with MYF and the youth choir."

Daisy's mother had been her best friend. She never went through the difficult stage that often gave girls an attitude about their mothers.

"I was lucky about Jake, too. He never had the money or time to get in too much trouble."

Lucas thought for a moment.

"We were fortunate too that alcohol was the only thing available to you and Jake."

Daisy started to protest but Lucas stopped her before she could.

"Hold on! I always knew what you were getting up to, and don't think I didn't. Your mother and I were glad when you and Jake had to give it up. Today people, including kids, can get anything they want, and the pushers have realized that the most money was to be made in heroin. Because it's so addictive."

Now Ed interrupted. "Time to call it a day, Lucas."

Daisy hugged her father and prepared to go back to her apartment.

"I'll see you in the morning," she said.

She took the umbrella she had brought from Lucas's office and stepped out into the storm. She opened the umbrella, held it in front of her face and body, and ran across the driveway toward the stairs leading to her apartment over the garage.

CHAPTER 18

Outside the rain blew sideways, fueled by tropical force winds. Daisy's umbrella was useless. She kept her head down and pushed on against the storm. When a sudden gust ripped the umbrella from her grip, she thought of returning to the house. Already at the halfway point, she decided to carry on. Her struggle with the wind seemed easier without the umbrella pulling on her. At the stairs she grabbed the railing and pulled herself the final steps to her apartment. The door was unlocked, as usual.

She shed her rain gear at the door. Her slacks were soaked so she took them off and left them by the door. Somehow her socks were also drenched so she shed them, too.

Straight to the bathroom Daisy turned on the shower. She was usually in a rush and took quick showers before going to work. Tonight, she wished for a tub she could fill with hot water and bubbles where she could soak until the water turned cold. She had to settle for shower water as hot as she could stand. She aimed the water at her neck which had been tense all day.

Drying with a soft towel she wrapped another around her head. In her bedroom she saw the cat curled up tight by her pillow. She was more presentable now. Her fur had dried and fluffed out to reveal a pretty white face sporting a black and orange mask.

"You still here, cat?" she said. "I'd forgotten all about you. Get to you in a minute."

She opened the top drawer of her chest of drawers and rummaged around. No clean pajamas or the oversized T-shirts she liked to sleep in. The He's Not Here shirt she had worn the night before was on top of her dirty laundry, so that would have to do.

"Now for you!"

The unwanted cat stood and slowly stretched. It sat down and looked at Daisy as if to say, "What now? What do you want me to do?"

The cat surrendered itself to Daisy's hands without biting or scratching. Instead, as Daisy held her close to her chest, it rubbed against Daisy's chin with its own and began to purr. The warmth of its small body was comforting. The stray purred louder as it kneaded with its claws on Daisy's arm.

"Don't think you can sweet talk me," Daisy said

marching to the door to put the cat out. When she opened it a blast of wind blew needles of rain on them both. Daisy slammed the door shut and set the cat down.

"Now, what to do with you. I can't very well put you out in that, can I?"

Daisy picked out a saucer and small bowl and took a small piece of deli turkey from the refrigerator. Holding it down so the cat could get a whiff, she said, "Follow me."

The cat followed obediently, all the way to the small bathroom. Daisy put the saucer with turkey on the floor. She filled the bowl with water and set it by the saucer. The cat gathered itself into a loaf shape and began to eat the deli turkey. Daisy closed the door.

She got her cell phone and told Siri to call Jake.

"Daisy!" Jake said when he answered the call. "Where are you?"

"Home. I had to get back to lock this cat in the bathroom where it couldn't make a mess all over the place." Daisy lied to forestall any lectures about the dangers of walking around during a tropical storm when debris would be flying around.

"What cat? You don't have a cat."

"It's not mine," she said. "It sneaked in somehow when I left for work this morning." She did not add that it was still in her apartment, albeit in the bathroom—or that she had fed it. "Enough of that—did you get the story to WLOS?"

"Yes. When I called to tell them it's coming, they told me it'll be on at eleven and then again tomorrow morning."

Daisy was silent.

"You okay?" Jake said.

"Yes, I'm not sure I'll put it on my vlog tonight, but have you sent that copy to me?" Daisy said.

"Sure did."

Daisy thanked him and went to turn on the TV. The news had not yet begun so she made a mug of hot chocolate before settling down on the couch.

Hearing a scratching sound coming from her bedroom she went to investigate and saw a tiny white paw reaching out from under the bathroom door. Opening it she said, "If that's how you feel, come on out. But don't think you're moving in here."

She and the cat sat side by side to watch the news. Daisy was impressed that Jake had added footage taken at the crash site. Daisy thought that made it much better, that the extra shots of the crashed Cessna were why WLOS rushed to air the piece tonight instead of holding it for tomorrow.

She also watched the weather. *Sunny tomorrow. I'll believe it when I see it. After I pick up my Jeep, I can go back and see if Louisa Simpson knows more than she let on.*

Turning of the television, she faced the petite stray and said, "All right, you can stay inside tonight, but only if you sleep on this couch. Understand?'

In response, the calico stood, circled around, and nestled against a velvety throw pillow.

"Fine!"

Daisy turned off the lights and went to her bedroom. Taking her laptop into bed, she opened her email and retrieved the video file Jake had sent. Like the report he had edited for WLOS, it was perfect, so she added it to her vlog.

She logged onto her Facebook page. After adding some still shots of the storm damage, she pasted a link to her vlog. She browsed the site for a bit and then went to Twitter to post the same photos and link to the vlog. She put the laptop on the floor, turned off the bedside lamp, and lay down to sleep.

Daisy had done a good day's work. As she fell asleep, the winds and rain raged on outside, scratching branches against her bedroom windows as the storm pushed through the Appalachian valley where Franklin slept.

In the morning Daisy found the calico lapping water from the toilet.

"Ugh, you have worn out your welcome."

She carried the cat out and put her on the landing where she immediately sat and began to lick a paw and use it to scrub her face clean. Daisy laughed at the nonchalant behavior and then went back in to dress for the day.

CHAPTER 19

The new car, a Jeep Compass Sport, was fully loaded. Red with tan seats, and a technology package which included Sirius.

Her old Jeep was a 2007 basic Wrangler, also red but well-worn. Her mother and father had given it to her for her senior year at Franklin High School and college. When she woke up on her seventeenth birthday, the Wrangler was parked in the driveway off the kitchen.

During her senior year Daisy picked up friends, including Jake, on the way to school. She let Jake take over driving so much that she finally just climbed over to the passenger seat when she pulled up to her house. It was this Jeep that carried them to the hemlock forest where they picnicked and made out on the blanket spread over the soft needles. It was in this Jeep that she returned to Franklin when her mother died.

It sat in the garage during her first year because freshmen at the University of North Carolina at Chapel Hill were not allowed to have cars. To get home during holiday and term breaks she would get a ride to Asheville where Lucas would pick her up.

The McLarens' plan had been to purchase a new car for Daisy upon graduation. They all thought she would get a job with the *News & Observer* in Raleigh. Then her mother died in the automobile accident, and Daisy returned to Franklin. The old Jeep was inextricably linked with her mother, and Daisy's incessant grief had allowed for no substitute.

Lucas and Daisy quickly completed the remaining paperwork, and Daisy was eager to get on the road.

"What's on your agenda today?" Lucas asked.

"I've got to do some more research and finish the story on de Soto's expedition through North Carolina. Chad wants it for the next print edition too. I hope to post more on my vlog by this afternoon. I'll see you for dinner."

She gave him a peck on his cheek and headed to her new car. She turned and said, "I love you."

"I love you too."

She switched the ignition on, pulled the automatic shift lever to reverse, and backed out of the parking space. The old Jeep had a six-speed manual transmission so the upgrade to automatic was nice. Sirius radio was already tuned to PopRocks, and "This Love" by Maroon

5 was playing. Daisy once had a huge crush on Adam Levine and still liked to see him on "The Voice." She sang along in her off-key way.

Daisy headed not to town but rather toward the Appalachian Highway. She had already determined that she would return to the Simpson Ruby Mine, and grill Louisa again about the plane crash. Her demeanor had changed dramatically when Daisy had mentioned the Walkers. She had latched on to the idea that they were involved in the mysterious plane crash too quickly.

Branches torn off and leaves blown about littered the roads between her home and the on ramp to I-64. Detour signs had been removed but one car remained with half an oak tree crushing it in two; the rest of the huge tree had been sawn into pieces small enough to be stacked on the other side of the road. Some traffic lights were still out. Duke Energy cherry pickers held crews working to restore power to neighborhoods.

Daisy knew that the Simpsons were crooked. A couple of mines still held rich lodes and did not have to enrich the buckets, but the Simpson Ruby Mine was not one of those. The Simpsons purchased cheap raw minerals in bulk from online sources, added them to buckets, and labelled them "Native." Tourists had much better odds of sifting out stones and getting their photo in the following week's ad for that mine in the Free Press. The more Simpson Ruby Mine appeared in the paper, the more the tourists came to try their luck.

Salting buckets of soil from the mine was quite a different kettle from dodgy dealings with the plane that crashed on the mountain, and Daisy was determined to discover the extent of that involvement.

She turned into the parking lot at the mine. Eric Simpson, the oldest son, was clearing the lot of storm debris, stacking it in piles to be tossed into surrounding woods later. Already overweight and having a surly look, Eric resembled his mother. The Simpson parents were like Jack Spratt and his wife. Simpson was skin and bones, and that skin was tough and leathery from outdoor work. Louisa Simpson was pasty-faced and obese from years of sitting at the counter.

Louisa was sitting at the counter as usual. "Back already? Heard you were in a bad accident t'other day. Had to get a new car?"

"Yes," Daisy replied. She shifted her feet. She really wanted to stay on the topic of the plane crash, not her accident in the tropical storm gully-washer. "Wasn't that bad. My old Jeep was totaled, but I wasn't hurt."

"You sure were lucky about that."

"I see Eric is helping clean up after the storm," Daisy said. "Did he go up when the plane crashed? I didn't see him in the crowd. But I thought I saw him heading back to your place after the plane blew up."

"Not my Eric," Louisa said. "He was still in bed. All my boys were. They're heavy sleepers. None of them get up before noon."

Daisy nodded and thought. "And Simpson, your husband?"

"Asleep, too. I'm the only one has to get up and work. Can't afford to miss customers."

Getting nowhere, Daisy changed tack and asked, "So, did you see anyone coming down the mountain? Any new customer stop by?"

"Nope. Slow morning. Everybody was busy with the crash."

Daisy decided to share her experience with Mr. Walker before the storm hit. "You know, the other day you seemed to think I should check out the Walkers, that they might know something about what the plane was doing out here."

"Yes. They're none too friendly."

"I went up there to ask," Daisy said slowly, "to see if they heard or saw anything that might point me in the right direction. Before I could ask, Walker told me to get off his land and fired a shot into the air."

"Now that gets me surprised," Louisa said. "They don't take to strangers, but I never heard of them threatening violence. You must've said something to get him riled up."

"No," Daisy insisted, "he didn't give me a chance."

"Well, I can't help you there. You getting another Coke?"

"Sure," Daisy said. She took out money to pay, took her Coke and left the shop.

CHAPTER 20

Back in town Daisy still had to take detours. Local contractors had cleared the roads of fallen trees, but most power lines were still down, and additional crews had to be called in from counties that the storm had bypassed. Orange traffic cones warned drivers to slow down in areas where Duke Energy workers were working on their lines and Morris Broadband crews were trying to restore cable service for TV and high-speed internet customers.

Although the sun cast a dazzling light on the fall leaves that had burst into full radiant color over the past days, Daisy knew more would have to pass before the chaos created by the storm could be returned to order.

Daisy's phone announced a call from an unknown

number. She let it ring through to voicemail, but, when she recognized Nathan Stark's voice recording the message, she answered. "Hello?'

"Is this Daisy McLaren?'

"Yes."

"Nathan Stark here," he said. "We met the other day with Sheriff Williams."

"Right?" Daisy wondered why he was calling.

"I need to get more information from you. I can come to your place."

"I'll just come to the Sheriff's office. I'm on my way to town."

Nathan hesitated, then said, "Why don't we meet at that café where we ran into you the other day? Stamey's?"

"Sure, I can be there in fifteen minutes."

As Daisy entered the parking lot, she saw Nathan sitting at one of the concrete tables in front of the cafe, alone. This day he wore a suit. To Daisy's eyes he looked good but intimidating. "Is this an official interrogation?" she said, taking a seat on a bench opposite him.

Nathan laughed. "No. I really just need to hear your take on things. Sheriff Williams told me that you think you saw a man running away from the plane just after it exploded. I'd like you to tell me more about that. Would you like a coffee or Coke?"

"No, thanks. Yeah, it seems like I'm the only one who saw him. But I'm sure he was there, running down the slope away from the crash and from all of us on the road."

Nathan jotted a few notes in his pad. "Can you describe what he looked like? Did he resemble anyone you know or have seen before?"

"No one I knew." Daisy shook her head. "Well, I thought it might have been Eric Simpson but his mother told me he had still been asleep."

She closed her eyes and took a slow breath.

"Take your time," Nathan said. "It's ok if you can't remember more details."

Daisy thought back to that day, the day before the tropical storm hit Franklin. When the fog burned off, the sky was a crisp blue. The rescue squad had arrived before she and Jake got there, and they were already beginning the attempt to save the pilot, but he was already dead. Jake was filming an onsite segment of Daisy standing on the road above the plane as the small craft exploded behind her. From where she stood, she saw the man running away. Now she understood why no one else had seen him. The fire set off by the explosion blocked their view.

"He looked like many men do in Franklin. Longish hair pulled back in a low ponytail. Blue jeans and a checked shirt, I mean a blue and black buffalo plaid shirt. He might have had a beard."

"What color hair?'

"Dark, dark brown."

"Was there anything else about the way he looked?"

Daisy shook her head. "He wasn't that big, regular weight and height from what I could see."

"What about the way he moved? Any peculiarities?"

"Yes." Daisy was excited to think how nimble he was. "He was running and hopping over rocks and branches as he ran, like he was used to being and running in the woods. He must be a local. At the least someone used to roaming around forests."

Nathan thanked Daisy for her help and asked her to call him if she thought of anything else.

"I'd like to ask you about Joe Taylor," Daisy said. "How is he doing?"

"I guess you haven't heard. Did you know him well?"

"I used to babysit him."

"I'm so sorry to tell you he passed away."

"No," Daisy cried.

She held back her emotions and asked, "Is it true he took heroin?"

"Unfortunately, yes. I hope the young people in Franklin can learn something from this. When we complete our work here, I can tell you how his death connects to the crash," Nathan said. "Off the record, I can tell you that our investigations into drug movement from Atlanta to the North Georgia and North Carolina mountains is the reason I came here. "

"So, the plane that crashed was carrying drugs?"

Nathan nodded. "We had word that a shipment of heroin, along with oxycontin, fentanyl and codeine, was expected. We'd hope to make arrests and seize the drugs at the airport, but then the plane crashed. As I said, this is strictly off the record, but I'm telling you in the hopes that you might hear something to help us find the drugs."

Daisy wondered if the mysterious second man she saw could have carried off the drugs.

"I'll be happy to help. Do you think the man I saw is a drug dealer?"

"I can't stress strongly enough that you need to keep any information about this man out of the paper. Keep it to yourself. However, if he figures in the group of people feeding this opioid epidemic, he is dangerous. He wouldn't hesitate to hurt you to keep you silent about it, if he thinks you know too much."

Daisy nodded contritely.

"I have to go but remember to call me first if you learn more."

She nodded again. The pieces of the puzzle were beginning to fit into a coherent depiction of the events preceding and following the crash.

Whoever the second man was, he could have chartered the plane to fly in a shipment of drugs. He probably knew the area and meant to fly over Ruby Mine Road to signal his partners that he was back from his mission so they could pick him up at the small-town airport.

That had to be it. Now all she had to do was discover the identity of that man.

CHAPTER 21

Downtown Daisy parked in front of the main branch of the First Citizens Bank. She had planned to go to the Macon County Historical Museum to do more research into the de Soto legend, but she decided first to ask around town about the plane crash and possible drug use in Franklin. Her conversation with Nathan Stark had merely confirmed what she already suspected, but it still unnerved her. She entered Books Unlimited. If anyone could help her sort everything out, it would be Lexie and Ralph, and she hoped they would help her without admonishing her to keep out of dangerous situations.

She had gone through high school with Lexie. When Daisy attended the University of North Carolina in Chapel Hill, Lexie enlisted in the Army. After completing basic training at Fort Bragg, she followed up with Advanced Individual Instruction for the Military Police.

Lexie met her husband Ralph while on Active Duty in Heidelberg. It didn't take long for Ralph to tell Lexie that he was in Military Intelligence, and Lexie often said that he was the "blabbiest" spy she had ever met.

Daisy considered how the truism, *opposites attract*, was especially apt when applied to this couple. Physically, Lexie was quick and fit, and one could imagine her bringing down a lawbreaker with no problem. Ralph was soft and intellectual, and one could easily imagine him sitting in a cubicle while monitoring transmissions from Slavic countries. He had a doctoral degree in Linguistics and had specialized in Russian. He spoke like a native from Moscow. Lexie enlisted after high school. The CIA recruited Ralph upon completing his degree. Lexie had dark skin and sported short dreadlocks. Ralph's skin burned after less than a morning in the sun.

What had brought them together? A shared love of reading. They got together after running into each other many times in the base bookstore.

When they moved to Lexie's hometown, it seemed logical to pool their resources to open a bookstore, a gamble that paid off. They purchased Books Unlimited and remodeled it to include a coffee shop. They offered both new and used books, magazines, and school supplies. This combination allowed them to succeed in a small town. They filled Saturday nights at the coffee shop with music lovers who came to hear one of the many local musicians and singers perform. Ralph was still called upon to work by contract for the government, more frequently as Putin became a more dangerous threat. At those times, Daisy helped at the shop.

"Daisy," Lexie said, "are you here to help? I hope so!"

Daisy looked around and saw a local teen, Keira Swan, at the coffee shop bar. "Where's Ralph?"

"I don't know," Lexie said. "He left in a hurry and said he'd be back soon, but that was over two hours ago. I can use some help."

"Sure thing." Daisy walked behind the counter with Lexie. "I wanted to ask you something anyway."

Daisy tore the plastic wrap covering the packing slip on a large box and used a box cutter to cut the tape sealing it closed. Looking at the list of novels in the box, she took them out and checked each one off. There were five copies each of *Cold Mountain* and its follow-up *Thirteen Moons*. The author Charles Frazier had gone to high school in Franklin, and his books set in the North Carolina mountains were always best sellers to the tourists. At the front of the store, there was a big display just for Frazier's books. Daisy placed the new copies on that rack.

Walking back to the counter, she began, "I'm still looking into the plane crash. Have you heard much about it?"

"Everybody's been talking about it, but I imagine you know all that, and more."

"Does anyone know why the plane was coming to Franklin?"

"Nope." Lexie lifted another box from the floor and placed it in front of Daisy. It contained an assortment of non-fiction. Books on precious stones and gem mining, legends of the mountains and the Cherokee Nation, folk tales, and remedies. A collection of Cherokee myths and legends collected by James Mooney caught her eye. One chapter was devoted to the early Spanish exploration of the Southeast.

"Lexie, I'd like to buy this book."

"Just take it and mark it off the inventory," Lexie said. "Consider it payment for today."

As a young man Mooney developed an interest in Native Americans, specifically in the Eastern Band of the Cherokee. Intrigued by the history of the Removal when about 800 people escaped and hid in the mountains until they could regroup in the Qualla Boundary, he devoted his life to studies of this group and other Native American tribes.

Daisy put the book with her things and returned to the thinking about the crash. "Do you think it could have been trying to get to the Walkers? Or the Simpsons? I saw a man fleeing from the crash, and, instead of coming up for help, he ran down the mountain toward the Simpson's mine."

"I wouldn't be surprised."

Daisy confided to Lexie about her intuitions. "I think one of those families might bring drugs into town. I think they might be bringing in a steady supply of marijuana and opioids like heroin. Did you hear about Joe Taylor?"

"I did hear about Joe." She tossed her head in Keira's direction. "They were friends. They got really close when Joe worked here after his parents sold the store to us."

Daisy and Lexie had flirted with marijuana in their teens, Daisy always fell asleep while Lexie stayed up listening to music on her CD player. Daisy doubted they would have tried anything stronger, even if anything stronger had been available.

Daisy opened her mouth to confide more in Lexie, but she remembered Nathan's orders and knew she had already said too much.

"Let me know if you hear more."

With that they worked silently, opening box after box until all the books had been inventoried and shelved.

Ralph still had not returned.

CHAPTER

22

Jake was waiting outside Drake and climbed into the passenger seat. "How about some tacos? Mi Casa's?" he said.

"Sounds good," she said, thinking that she had given him a rough time lately with all her teasing and mentioning Nathan Stark whenever she had a chance. She was not crazy about fried Mexican food that often upset her stomach, but she did love a good burrito.

"I went to see Lexie this morning. Did you hear about Joe Taylor?"

"Yeah, I'm glad that shit wasn't around when we were young. You would have tried it for sure!"

"I would…" Daisy spluttered. Then she saw Jake's smirk--he was laughing at her. Tit for tat time. "Seriously. I talked with Nathan this morning, and he told me that's why he's here, to investigate how heavy drugs are making their way here from Atlanta. He thinks the Cessna was probably making a run."

"He does, does he?" Jake growled, his hackles rising. He took a deep breath. "You think your second man got away with the drugs, they ended up on the street, and Joe bought some, used them, and died. Have you told Stark this?"

"Uh huh." Daisy nodded. "He thinks I might be right about a second person in the plane. He thinks they might have gotten away with the drugs. After I left him, I realized that he had a backpack, but it wasn't on his back. He was carrying it."

"So, you met with Stark? After all Lucas and I have warned you about keeping away from this! I hope Stark also told you to leave it to professionals like him and Ben."

When Daisy did not reply, Jake said, "You just have to look for trouble, don't you? Drug smugglers are dangerous people. They wouldn't think twice about getting rid of you if you get in their way."

"I don't plan to get in their way!" Daisy said. "It's just irritating that you think I would do that. But I have to report on it. That's my responsibility."

"You could do that by talking with Ben. He'd tell you exactly what I'm saying, and you know it."

At Mi Casa they got out and did not talk again until they had their order and were at a table. Daisy wanted to change the subject so she asked if Jake would help her film a story about the Nikwasi Mound located on Depot Street.

"According to the legend, that's where the Cherokee attacked de Soto and rescued the princess. They chase de Soto and his men north toward Wayah Bald, and it's said that on the way de Soto had to abandon a small cannon, all that remained of the artillery brought from Spain. There's supposed to be a cannonball in the Museum. I'd like to find the cannon."

"I can help you with that. I'm off Friday so how about then? And in the meantime, if you have to go back on Ruby Mine, I'll go with you. Agreed?"

Daisy did a half-hearted nod to Jake and assumed she was saying, "Maybe.

The Macon County Historical Society and Museum houses artifacts and memorabilia from the Stone Age through modern times. Some came from a few small archaeological digs sponsored by a Southwestern Community College history professor. The majority came from residents.

Fifth graders in Franklin went to the museum each year. This first major attempt to inculcate in the young residents with an appreciation and understanding of the ancient and varied history of their town flew by as most of the students were mentally swooping down on the Main Street Coffee and Tea for an ice cream fix. Daisy was enthralled.

The fifth-grade outing began in the small park on the corner where the students sat on the grass. The park at that time was essentially an empty grassy lot. Once the students were seated and quieted, the museum's curator Terry Gibson told them about the museum, its history, and how the collection had grown. He invited them to bring anything "old" they found to him for a free evaluation.

"Once you enter the museum, you must keep your hands to yourselves," he said. "The glass cases are locked (a lie), and an alarm will go off (another lie) if you touch the glass or the locks. Any questions?"

The students were then invited to purchase any of the books or items that the Historical Society sold to keep the museum afloat.

At the beginning of the eighth-grade field trip to the museum, they were told about the lies, but their history teacher told them that he would drop their grade a full letter if they touched anything in the museum. That worked and the museum survived the field trip with flying colors.

At the end of the fifth-grade field trip, Daisy had stopped at the counter as other students rushed out to regroup at the Coffee and Yogurt Shop. She purchased a replica of a wampum pouch. Jake had also stopped at the counter. He bought a plastic Cherokee tomahawk.

Daisy began her visit as she had done on both of those school trips although she stopped in the yogurt shop for a Chai Latte before going to sit on a park bench installed by the Franklin Garden Club.

She wanted to see the collection of Cherokee findings. She was especially interested to see Margaret Siler's famous cannonball that was found in her field north of town. She had given this to the museum as proof of de Soto's visit to Franklin in the 1500s. A professor at Western Carolina had disputed her claim. As far as Daisy knew, someone decided to trust the academic rather than Margaret Siler and history was changed, but Daisy could not recall seeing any tactile proof of the professor's assertion.

Daisy tossed her latte cup in the trash can and entered the Museum.

Terry was at the counter to the right of the front door, as usual. "Good afternoon, Daisy," he said. "What's up?"

"I'm working on a story about the legend of de Soto. A lot of people still believe the Spaniards and Cherokee fought over the princess by the Nikwasi Mound. That the Spanish were defeated."

"Thought that was settled, that they went through Asheville and straight out west. Let's see, where did they say they crossed the ridge?" Terry was questioning his own memories but hoping that Daisy would answer.

"I know," she did, "but what was his proof?"

"Well," Terry began to recite the legend, but Daisy cut him off. "I know all that. Do you have any old Spanish coins from de Soto's time?"

"No, ma'am."

Daisy glowered. "But you do have the cannonball Mrs. Siler said was left by de Soto in one of her family farm's fields? Can I see that?"

They walked down the aisle on the left side of the museum, where items dating from the Stone Age to

World War I were housed. They passed cases filled with arrowheads and spearheads carved from flint, obsidian, or other hard rocks. Weapons made of bone and antler. Household items used in cooking or preparing hides for tents or clothing.

More display cases held things used by the early British traders and settlers.

As they approached the end of the row, the cannonball sat with a copy of Margaret Siler's book and a newspaper article about the theory that the cannonball came from a Civil War skirmish.

"There she is," Terry said. "What do you think?"

"It's so small."

CHAPTER 23

Daisy plopped the heavy book she had purchased at the bookstore down on the kitchen table and plopped herself on the couch by Ed. Dinner, a casserole of some sort, was in the oven. The 6 o'clock news sports and weather was on the tv.

"Any more storms coming?" Daisy asked.

Ed said, "Not until maybe next week. Laura Tomkins said she's watching a tropical storm and..."

"...will have more on it at eleven." Daisy and Ed quoted together. Lucas smiled at them from his seat at the table.

"Great," Daisy said. "Jake and I have to film a report at the mound tomorrow. Good to know I won't need my umbrella."

"Make us a salad, Daisy," Ed said.

Daisy liked this time of day when she got to Lucas's early enough to help with dinner. While Ed got out a trivet and set the casserole on the table to cool, Daisy put a tray of homemade rolls in the oven to warm. Then she retrieved her favorite wooden salad bowl.

No matter what the greens or additions, she always began her salads the same way. The same way her mother had taught her. She peeled a clove of garlic and sliced it in two. She rubbed the clove sections all around the bottom of the bowl, first one and then the other. Next came an extra-virgin olive oil and salt, which she lightly rubbed around the bowl.

Then, the greens. She took a large bag of arugula purchased at the farmer's market and pulled out three large handfuls and dumped them in the prepared bowl. Using the wooden salad spoon and fork, she tossed until the arugula was well coated. Keeping it simple, she squeezed lemon juice over the salad, grated parmesan on top, threw in a handful of pine nuts, and tossed it all again.

Daisy took the rolls from the oven, put them in a basket, and then took salad and rolls to the table to join her father and Ed, who were already digging into their meal, Chicken Alfredo Casserole, with pressed tofu substituting for the chicken.

Lucas asked, "How's the car? Any problems with it?"

"It's great, Daddy. I hadn't realized how clunky my old Jeep had become."

They continued with small talk during the meal.

"Daddy, can I talk with you after we wash up? In private?"

"I can take care of all this, Daisy. You go on and visit with your dad."

Daisy and Lucas went to sit on the rocking chairs on the side screened porch. Three rocking chairs with wood frames and cowhide seats lined up in a row facing the garden. An old metal glider backed to the end screen opposite the screened door that led down to the garden.

As Daisy grew up, the McLarens spent many evenings rocking and talking on the porch and many Sunday afternoons reading the Sunday newspapers from Atlanta and Raleigh. Since her mother's death, they rarely came out here. Too many memories of times of joy and of sorrow had been spent on this porch. Daisy and Lucas had avoided thinking of them all.

"I met with Nathan Stark today. You know, the FBI agent who is looking into the plane crash. He called me to meet him."

"What did he want with you? Hadn't you already told Ben everything you know?"

"Yes, but Nathan wanted to know more about the man I saw running away. I told him everything I recalled about the man, how he looked. I'm sure I had already given Sheriff Williams all those details."

"So why come to you?"

"I think his real motive was to warn me off. He told me that he's in Franklin to get evidence on a gang of drug smugglers. They surely sold the heroin that killed

Joe Taylor. He said they are extremely dangerous and told me not to print any more about the crash or my suspicions, and not to even talk about them—with anyone. I figured that didn't include you or Jake."

"Then you have to do what he said."

"I will. That is, I won't write anything about the other man or drugs, but it will look strange if I don't do any follow-up on just the crash. People would start asking me about it."

"You could be right, but if you insist on writing more about it don't include any of your hypotheses."

"I'll just work on a final article about the crash and then get back to my story about de Soto. I just wanted you to know about Nathan Stark. I know you won't repeat any of this."

"Daisy, I know you're a grown woman, but I wouldn't be doing my duty as your father if I didn't add my words of caution to his. I've seen the people who end up in court for selling heroin and other hard drugs. The small dealers. They're a rough bunch. The big-time distributors have to be ruthless to keep those in line, half of the small dealers are junkies themselves. Now I don't want to preach at you but do what Stark has said. He knows what he is talking about."

Daisy was still too young to comprehend her own mortality. She knew death. The pain of persistent and inescapable loss had been driven home when her mother died. She had worried about Lucas when the first symptoms of post-polio appeared. Then Ed came, and Daisy could see her father getting stronger. She no longer feared that she would lose him. He was not an old man in her eyes, not like her grandparents had been before they passed away. He still had a vigorous approach to each new day.

Still, she believed that death was meant for old people. No one in her high school or in her group of friends in Chapel Hill had died. It was unthinkable that she might die young. Or that Jake would.

Lucas compared Daisy often to her mother, but Daisy shared with him a physical strength and an undying need to discover the truth about the world. They also shared a desire to protect each other from the harshness of reality.

With this desire in mind Daisy said, "I promise."

CHAPTER 24

The stray cat was waiting for her at the top of the stairs and rubbed around her legs as she unlocked the door. She rushed past Daisy and went straight to the small kitchen.

"I think you're exactly right, cat," said Daisy. Having the small creature anticipating her homecoming and waiting to greet her was nice, reassuring after a long day. Daisy walked over to bend down and scratch the cat's head. She provided fresh water and cat food to some bowls.

She opened the freezer and took out a container of Cherry Garcia for herself. Ice cream was her most effective comfort food and spooning Cherry Garcia out of the container was the fastest path to comfort.

She sat on the couch and turned on the television. Ignoring her own food, the cat jumped on the couch beside her and stared at Daisy and then at the Cherry Garcia.

"Do you want some of this?"

The cat made a purripping sound that sounded to Daisy like yes and rubbed against her arm. Daisy put a dollop in the Ben & Jerry's lid and put it next to the cat.

"You're a persistent little thing, aren't you? I wish you could talk." Daisy took a big spoonful. "I need to understand why my mother was on that road. You know? Where she died."

The cat stared at Daisy and then returned to lapping ice cream.

"I know that she wouldn't have gone there without a good reason. Nobody lives on that road, so she had to have been either meeting someone or looking for something. I wish my dad could be honest with me. I know he's holding back something important."

The news came on and Daisy turned the volume up. There was the usual local news. No reports of drugs or overdoses. A lot about the upcoming Thanksgiving Festival with a video of the past festivals and announcements about the many church services and homecomings for people of all ages. Then sports and finally the weather.

Laura Tomkins was on again, "We're keeping a close eye on a Cat One hurricane headed toward the Caribbean. If the eye makes landfall in Florida, it will probably then turn north and pass us by. However, if it goes into the warm waters of the Caribbean, we can expect it to build in strength and size and impact our area. At the very least be prepared for severe rain and wind by early next week. Scientists are attributing the late and severe hurricane season to global warming."

Daisy told the cat, "I guess I better find out what's happening on that mountain before the next storms get here. What do you think?"

The cat curled like a croissant next Daisy and purred herself to sleep. Daisy turned the television off and took up the heavy red book she had brought home that contained reprints of Mooney's collections, *Myths of the Cherokee* and *The Sacred Formulas of the Cherokees*.

James Mooney was an American ethnologist at the end of the nineteenth century. Under the auspices of the Bureau of American Ethnology, he compiled a list of Native American tribes. Mooney found it necessary to live among the people to learn the language, so he dwelled for several years with the Cherokee in Oklahoma and in the Qualla Boundary of North Carolina.

As the richness of their history and mythology revealed itself, his research took on a depth not before known among students of Native American life. Fortunately, through his education he had learned the importance of recording everything he learned. His writings and collected artifacts have been preserved in various departments of the Smithsonian Institution.

It was hard to tell how many pages were in the tome. They were numbered as in the original publications of the books, but she figured that it contained at least 1,000 pages. She carried the book and placed it on her nightstand while she changed for bed and brushed her teeth. When she returned from the bathroom the cat was already waiting by her pillow.

"I guess you can look at it with me," she said and crawled under the covers.

Using the table of contents for the first of Mooney's books, she located a section on the period of Spanish exploration which began when de Soto set out from Cofitachiqui in May 1540. The queen of the tribe had welcomed the Spaniards at first, but de Soto's arrogance had angered her, and she denied them assistance for their explorations.

De Soto, intent on finding gold and silver mines, responded to her refusal by seizing her and forcing her to serve as their guide herself. Her presence ensured the cooperation and aid from her subjects as they passed through her territories. Rather than taking de Soto directly to the land he sought, she took a vagabond route through the mountains until with the help of three of her subjects who had been taken as slaves.

The rumor that de Soto heard of her escape was that she had taken one of these men as her husband was returning to her land, but this was not confirmed in the chronicles. De Soto was angry that she had escaped, but even angrier that she had taken with her a small box of pearls he had intended to take as his own.

After giving an overview Mooney returned to the beginning to add details about the queen, the route they took, why they thought there were gold mines to be found in the mountains. Each iteration of the story added the names of more tribes, town, and rivers.

Daisy dropped the book on the floor by her bed.

"My head is swimming," she told the cat who was purring contently beside her. "Do you feel like getting a midnight snack?'

The calico did not even lift her head but continued to purr in her sleep as Daisy went to the other room. On the way home she had purchased a dishpan and a bag of kitty litter. She carried them to the bathroom and set up the litter box for the cat.

Remembering she had already brushed her teeth, Daisy settled on a glass of water and stepped outside to her small landing to drink it.

The night sky was filled with stars. Daisy found Orion, the hunter, and satisfied went inside to sleep.

CHAPTER 25

At daybreak, a dense fog imbued the woods with soft tints of saffron, rose, and the palest yellow. The cat attempted to wake Daisy up early by gently touching her nose with her paw. Daisy turned away from her and pulled the covers up tight to her chin. She had stayed up to late reading about the early explorations of the Southeast by de Soto and others and was unable to rouse herself. She felt the cat gently pricking her back and then sliding against her under the sheet and blanket. Snug in bed they both went back to sleep.

When she woke again, the fog had burned off. The sky provided a glorious azure background on which the trees had painted from a palette loaded with the bright yellows, reds, and oranges of tulip poplar, maple, and dogwood. The deep reds and rusty reds of mature oaks would come later, and with their turning to brown, snow would fill in spots of earth.

The cat lay still under the covers and snuggled tight against Daisy's legs. Daisy sat up and pushed the covers so that only the cat's head showed. As she rubbed it between the ears, it purred. This time the cat preferred to linger in the snug and warm bed.

"Good morning, cat. Have you used your nice litter box?" The cat just purred louder. Daisy went to investigate. The litter had been scratched around to cover signs of feline activity. It had been swiped around so vigorously that some litter went on the floor. Daisy fetched a broom and dustpan to sweep up the spills. Now curious about the activity the cat crept out from under the covers. She sat back on her haunches and licked her furry white belly.

"I hope we don't have to move that," she told the cat. "You'll have to use it correctly, you know, if you plan to stay on here. We don't dare have a flap for you that possums and raccoons are sure to use as well. Let's get breakfast."

At that the cat leaped from the bed and tail up, sauntered into the kitchen.

Daisy popped some English muffins into the toaster. The cat sat simply looking at its water bowl.

"What's the matter now? Something wrong with the water?" Picking it up, Daisy saw bits of dust on the surface. "Right picky, aren't you? I'd have thought a stray would be grateful just to have water in a dish."

She took up one bowl and filled it with fresh water. She crumbled am English muffin in another bowl and put both in front of the cat.

She Keuriged her coffee, buttered the muffins, and carried both to her bedroom. She quickly showered and ate while dressing.

Mooney's book lay still on the floor where Daisy had dropped it before falling asleep. She thought about what she had read. Although Franklin was never specifically mentioned, Mooney confirmed that a captive princess had led de Soto on a random route through the mountains, so it was still conceivable to Daisy that they had ventured into Macon County. Left unconfirmed was whether or not the princess ever made it back to Cofitachiqui. Still missing was the box of pearls.

Daisy was hooked on the legend of de Soto in North Carolina and of the possible connection to the Nikwasi Mound. She was eager to read more. In the table of contents, a myth of *The Spirit Defenders of Nikwasi* was listed. She thought the defenders could be the Cherokee braves who aided their princess with her escape.

Daisy had learned from her attorney father to be a skeptic, to doubt stories that were not backed by evidence. Essential in Lucas's trial work, the same philosophy guided Daisy through her career in journalism and had prevented her from making substantial factual errors in her reporting. She was careful to attribute statements of facts to their speakers. This had saved her from potentially embarrassing situations.

At the same time Lucas has taught her that even the

grandest of lies contained some amount of truth. She learned to explore what she considered to be false rumors to get at that grain of truth. One of those explorations had given her the biggest story of her reporting at the *Daily Tar Heel*, a series of articles about methamphetamine use on campus and the chemistry doctoral candidate who had used his laboratory to produce the meth. She had won first place in the Hearst Investigative Reporting competition for this series.

Daisy regarded mythologies the same way she had viewed lies—many held some truth within the fiction. She had grown listening to the Cherokee myths. Her mother had told her many of them as bedtime stories. She wept when she heard of the Wolf Man who could not go back to living as a man and so perished. She loved the story of the woman whose love of strawberries brought her home to her husband.

Many of the myths tried to explain how the world was made, how the sun, stars, and moon began. Stories about how a pesky rabbit was outsmarted were among her favorites. She learned of Br'er Rabbit in school, but she preferred the tales about the trickster "The Rabbit" told her by her mother.

She viewed the Cherokee legends and traditional stories about interactions with white men the same way she regarded the myths. The Cherokee braves and women always came out well in these versions of history. Daisy doubted that was always the case, but she granted that the stories that were told and retold had been selected because of that point of view while others were left by the mountain trails.

Daisy put these thoughts out of her mind as she gathered her bag and keys to leave. She put more fresh water out for the stray cat and left her apartment. She needed to have a single-minded purpose for this was the day Daisy had decided to return to the Walker place and find out why they were so secretive, but first she wanted the explore the area where her mother had died.

CHAPTER 26

The lanes on the highway were clear of storm debris. The distant mountains to the west were concealed in a gray mist of not yet burned-off fog and clouds which had not cleared the mountaintops. The sky above the eastern peaks was Carolina blue. Daisy had never feared the mountains surrounding Franklin, but today she was afraid of what she might find in those wooded ridges and hollows.

Daisy took an exit just before the Ruby Mine Road exit. She drove along a frontage road until she came to an unmarked dirt road that wove its way up the mountain. When the government required that every road be named, no one was living on the road to claim it and name it. Most people forgot the road was even there, but it was never far from Daisy's thoughts. She had told no one, not even Jake, that she often drove up there to sit in her car and think about her mother. This was the road on which her mother had her fatal accident.

Daisy's father had never given an answer that satisfied her curiosity about what her mother was doing on such a deserted road. Alice McLaren was a social worker. At various times Lucas suggested that she was looking for a house that had been overlooked in census counts, that she made a wrong turn, and even that she was checking out some land that they thought about buying.

None of those made any sense to Daisy. Her mother had lived all her life in Macon County. She had traveled the county roads to visit families for 35 years. She ensured that children went to school with the supplies they needed. That they received necessary vaccinations and health care. That mothers received prenatal care and were able to deliver their babies in safe conditions.

Alice was known for her generosity. She often purchased with her own money clothing, shoes, and warm winter coats when families had no money for those. She arranged summer camp and swimming lessons for children whose families were not able to afford them.

She cared for the living, sat with the dying, and never seemed to tire of these responsibilities. She was persistent and indefatigable and, if ever a person could be described as a force of nature, it was Alice McLaren.

Daisy drove to the top of the deeply-rutted road and stopped. Perhaps she could find the cabin rumored to be there. She put on her hiking boots, grabbed a walking stick, and set out to the east and north. The laurel thickets and fallen trees impeded her progress. She walked slowly and carefully, using the walking stick in front of each step to check for copperheads and timber rattlers that would still be out on this warm Indian summer day. Receiving a bite while alone in these woods could be fatal.

She meandered through the forest always checking her compass to keep moving in the same general direction. Coming upon a creek, she took out the topo map to check her position. She sat down on a fallen tree to drink water from her canteen. The woods were silent, and she thought how the woods were always dead silent when man entered them. Even squirrels froze from fear they were the prey for that day, for that hunter.

As a girl she enjoyed sitting still and quiet in the woods until life began to stir around her once more. On hikes with her parents, she often managed to talk them into leaving her while they climbed on to an overlook or some other goal. As the sound of their steps grew faint, the chirps and barks of the wildlife around her began. She heard the rustlings and scratching of small mammals like squirrels and chipmunks. Rarely she heard the huffed warning of a bear.

She could see how the creek must follow below a ridge leading back to just above where she had parked. Exploring the area at a higher elevation would be enough searching for that day. When she had rested and felt replenished, she stepped into the creek bed. Walking in it would be easier than along its banks where laurel and blackberries grew thick.

She soon came to a still of the kind used in the early twentieth century. The moonshine produced in these stills often led to blindness or kidney disease in its users. Bootleggers still in the business had replaced the lead radiators once used for condensation with copper tubing.

After taking a few pictures, she continued until she thought she was just north of the old road where she had parked. Using her binoculars, she studied the woods all around to see if there were any signs of a cabin.

Seeing none she cautiously made her way down again through the laurel "ivy," as the old folks still called the thickets that grew in the dense shade of mountain forests, until she came to her Jeep.

As she was about to climb in, she heard a clattering sound behind her, like rocks tumbling over each other down a slope. She jerked around to locate the source of the noise but saw nothing. She tried to shrug it off, thinking that it must have been some unseen animal that had scampered away frightened by the noise of its own making, but she could not help but think someone had been watching her.

Daisy tried her cell phone but had no service. She was eager to get away. Backing her car all the way down the road would be impossible for her as it was miles to the frontage road. Tossing her gear in the back, she had no choice but to back down the road until she either had cell phone reception or found a space wide enough to make a Y-turn. When she finally reached a spot with bars on her phone, she completed the turn and drove away. Relieved she drove down the mountain towards home.

CHAPTER 27

The morning's activities had stressed Daisy's body and mind, and she was no closer to discovering what her mother had been doing on the remote road. What had become clear as the water in the mountain's spring-fed creeks was that she had not been alone. What was not clear was the reason they chose to hide their presence from her.

Daisy went straight to her apartment over the garage. The cat slept on the warm cable modem. It looked up but did not rise. "If you were a dog, you'd rush over to jump up and greet me. You're utterly useless."

She tossed her bag on the couch, took off her coat and did the same with it. She stomped to the refrigerator and peered in to see what comfort food she might find.

No ice cream. Nothing really except skim milk. She took the carton and poured herself a glass. Now the cat was entwining itself around her legs while purring loudly.

"I guess you want some?" Daisy poured some in the empty food bowl. She finished her milk and once again picked up the Mooney collection to glean more information about the Spanish in North Carolina. She found the book by Margaret Siler which her father had given her and opened it to the same legend.

Siler had written that the Spaniards had captured an Indian princess, while Mooney referred to her as a queen. Furthermore, Siler said her name was Chualiah, or the Anglicized pronunciation and spelling of Xualla; in Mooney she has no given name.

Both chroniclers mentioned treasures. De Soto bristled at the fact that not only had she escaped but also that she had absconded with her box of pearls that de Soto coveted. Chualiah gifted de Soto with a pearl necklace and in return he gave her a large ruby set in a ring, according to Siler. Daisy wanted to know more about the treasure—what it consisted of and what happened to it. The thought that this mysterious treasure could be linked to the plane crash tickled her imagination.

She set the books on couch and went to shower and change before going back to the Walkers' place.

When she stepped out of the shower, her damp feet picked up granules of kitty litter scattered on the tiles.

"Cat," she screeched. "We're going to find where you came from and send you back—today."

In her bedroom the little stray was nowhere to be

seen.

Daisy dressed quickly. Refreshed and somewhat restored, she was ready to go out.

When she opened the door, the stray cat dashed past her and down the stairs.

CHAPTER 28

Daisy turned off at the Ruby Mine Road exit. The Watson's mine was open for business, but she passed by. Farther along the road the wreckage of the Cessna remained, but visiting that on foot was a project she had already scheduled for another day. The authorities had finished searching the area and had found no evidence that a second man had been involved. Daisy planned to start at the place where the small Cessna had crashed and hike down to the Simpson Ruby Mine. If he had left tracks, litter, or any other signs, Daisy would find them. Looking for animal tracks in snow or mud had been a favorite pastime as she grew up in the mountains.

That would have to wait for another day. On this

day she was determined to explore the Walkers' mountain homestead and find evidence of their drug sales.

She stopped and got out of the Jeep when she reached the spot where she had totaled her old Wrangler. Whether she thought of it as a dream or a vision, her experience of seeing de Soto and the native princess had seemed real. She still shuddered to remember the face of the Cherokee warrior with his face painted red for battle. Later she would read Mooney's account more carefully. Perhaps he had planted additional clues about the missing box of pearls. That would certainly intrigue her readers.

Daisy saw the scars left on the rock when she crashed. As she traced them with her fingertips, she recalled how relieved she was when Jake's face replaced that of the Cherokee. Looking over the steep drop across the road from the boulder she crashed into, she felt lucky to still be among the living.

Daisy got back in the Jeep and turned on her cellphone. She wanted to find the last spot where she would have reception in case she needed to call for help. Jake would be furious if he knew what she was doing, and her father would not be pleased. The bars disappeared so she turned onto a pull-off close by. She locked the car and started the hike up the deeply rutted dirt and gravel road. She carried her phone to take pictures to document whatever she might find. Daisy had learned that a cell phone provided a false sense of security in this isolated part of the world but having it along was better than nothing.

I've got to get in that cabin. But first I'll see what that path leads to. She thought about the well-worn path that seemed to lead only to a junkyard. *That must be where they keep the drugs. Walker doesn't work. There are no signs of farming or anything else. He's got to be making money from drugs.*

Daisy saw the open area of the homestead ahead. Hoping to come out right near the path she had seen, she left the road and continued her climb through the woods. The laurel thickets and rock outcroppings slowed her down. She could not risk a fall. She wound her way around the thickets until she came to the clearing and saw the well-trodden path.

Daisy stayed in the woods as she made her way closer. She came to the clearing and looked around for signs of life. She neither saw nor heard a soul. She could clearly see the yard and the open porch. No dogs in sight. Their presence could have ruined her entire plan.

She walked a few steps out of the woods and stopped. Still no sign of the dogs so she figured it was safe to proceed. Quickly she darted across the clearing and entered the path. She crept along slowly, passing by junked cars and trucks until she came to the structure. It was a small log cabin, probably built by the original settler to live in while the larger cabin was being built.

When Daisy approached the door, she got a whiff of a smell like rotting garbage. The door was fastened with a latch string system. Daisy pulled the string and felt the latch being raised to unbolt the door. She cautiously pushed it open and entered slowly. The one room of the hut had no windows. It took a few moments for her eyes to adjust to the darkness. She saw a wooden table with two chairs and an unlit lantern and in the far corner a bed.

Daisy turned on the flashlight on her phone and closed the door behind her. The air reeked with the stench of decay. Shining the light around, she saw nothing else in the room. She covered her nose as she approached the bed. The light revealed what seemed to be someone under the coverlet.

"Hello?" she called out.

There was no answer. She walked slowly over, and still shining the beam of light on the figure, she lifted the cover. There lay the body of Caleb Walker. She knew him immediately even though his face was bloated. Swarms of flies filled the room and were alighting on his face. She covered her nose and mouth to suppress the gag reflex that was building in the back of her throat. She turned her back on his body and breathed deeply as she had been taught to halt the panic building rapidly in her body.

She remembered she could take pictures and turned back to the bed. She noticed that the pillow beside him bore the imprint of a head and that the covers on that side of the bed had been tossed back as though someone had recently climbed out. She took several photos of Caleb, the room, and the pillow and covers beside his body. Satisfied she put her camera away and prepared to leave.

Daisy hoped to leave as quietly as she came. Never

had she imagined that Caleb was dead, and she certainly had not expected to stumble upon his corpse. Who had murdered him? The Walkers were the only family living on this lonely summit. Could they have killed their only son? Her thoughts ran to Jasmine. Could she also be dead?

Daisy tried desperately to control her breath, but her racing mind threatened to paralyze her. She had to leave immediately. Once she reached her car, she could use the cell to call the sheriff.

A loud shriek abruptly filled the air around her. Daisy went numb at the sound. She was unable to move until she heard someone crashing towards her. She covered her head as she turned to face Mrs. Walker towering over her with arms upraised. She could not imagine why or how Caleb's mother had killed him, but Daisy was not ready to die.

CHAPTER 29

"Nooo," the ghoulish figure screamed at Daisy. "Get away from him." She pushed Daisy to the floor and climbed on the bed beside the remains to embrace her child.

"Don't be scared, Caleb. Mama's here now." She lay next to him and placed her arm over his cold and dead body.

Daisy remained on the floor. She tried to stand but, almost fainting, collapsed instead. She broke out in a cold sweat. Nausea overwhelmed her. She turned her face toward the wall and, no longer able to control her reflexive actions, vomited at last. Throughout her physical reactions to the scene unfolding before her, her mind still raced.

Caleb? When did he die? How could Retta Walker lie down with his body? It was clear that Caleb had been kept here for several days. Daisy wiped the vomit that clung to her mouth and covered her mouth and nose to block the sickening stench of the smell of death. Who else knew about this?

As if on cue Walker, shotgun at the ready, rushed into the room behind his wife. He halted by the door when he saw Daisy sprawled on the floor next to the bed where his son's body lay. In disbelief she looked up at him then rested her head on her arms. Walker walked over and bent down to hold Daisy's head gently.

He stood quietly until she turned her head and looked up at him.

"Can you get up now?"

Daisy nodded. He held his hand out to her. Daisy took it. Supporting her other side under the arm, he helped her stand.

Daisy questioned him with her eyes.

"Let's get you in the house first. I'll explain everything."

As they left Mrs. Walker with the body of her son for the time being, Daisy glanced back at the tableau and felt a deep sorrow for this mother who had lost her only son. She leaned into Walker who now held her gently as they walked slowly to the old homestead cabin where thetwo dogs waited silently.

CHAPTER 30

As they approached the log cabin Daisy shivered at the memories of Caleb's body and of Mrs. Walker charging at her. As surreal as it seemed, she knew it was all too real. A multitude of questions called for answers, but Daisy feared the answer to only one. Who killed Caleb? She shuddered to think it might be the man who was helping her now, the man who was shepherding her into his house.

The only other suspect was Mrs. Walker. Could a mother kill her child? When attacking Daisy, she certainly seemed insane. Perhaps she was psychotic and, not recognizing that he was her son, murdered him.

Of course, there remained the mystery of the plane crash and why it had been flying close to this remote farm. Could Caleb have been in league with the drug smugglers Daisy believed were on the plane? She could not reconcile her memories of the boy she knew in school with a criminal. He had been studious and gentle.

As she and Walker drew near the log cabin, she grew faint and collapsed further against him. He helped her inside and lowered her carefully onto the sofa. She leaned over to rest her head on the sofa's arm and closed her eyes.

"Would you like a drink of water? Or a soda?" Walker asked.

She nodded.

"I'll get you some, and then I'll phone Sheriff Williams."

"You have a telephone?" Daisy asked weakly.

"Yes, over the internet, VOIP."

Daisy thought nothing could shock her after the events of the day. She had expected this cabin to be like all the others she knew around Franklin, but as she looked around, she saw a thoroughly modern living room. She recognized the furniture as expensive, maybe Ethan Allen. The heart-of-pine floors were finished in place. Daisy, even though still in a daze, could see it was a beautiful version of an interior decorator's idea of rustic. The centerpiece of the room was the original stone hearth and fireplace where a cozy fire burned.

Daisy could not decide which was stranger: this house or the scene she had just left in the small log cabin. She certainly had not expected to find either. This living room did not fit with the image Walker had cast when he stood on the decrepit porch and fired his shotgun to scare her off when she had last approached the property.

She could not imagine that either Walker or his wife would have decorated their home in this manner. She could not imagine them hiring a decorator. Where could they have gotten the money for a project this big? The more she learned about this family, the more questions she had.

Having seen his wife protecting Caleb's body in the other cabin, Daisy understood why he wanted to keep people away. What she did not understand was why he had not gotten help for his wife, why he kept his wife a prisoner on this mountaintop.

Walker returned bearing a glass of water and a mug. "I made you some coffee too."

Daisy hesitated to take anything he offered. He placed them on the low table before her.

"I'm going to call Ben Williams now."

As she listened in to his side of the conversation, she relaxed. When she heard him ask for an ambulance as well, she picked up the water and gulped it down. She picked up the steaming mug and held it between her hands to warm them. The shock of the experience had chilled her to the core.

Walker hung up the phone and returned his attention to Daisy.

"The sheriff is on the way."

Daisy felt herself to be soiled, stained by the gruesome discovery in the cabin.

"I need to take a shower," Daisy murmured.

"Sure. Let me get you some towels."

Daisy followed Walker down the hall and entered the bathroom.

"There's shampoo on the counter you can use, and toothbrush and toothpaste. Those are extras we keep on hand for when Jasmine can come visit," he said as he handed her a stack of white, fluffy towels. "Do you need anything else right now?"

Daisy shook her head.

"I'll leave you to it then."

Walker closed the door behind him. Daisy moistened the toothbrush and spread a thick line of paste across the bristles. She vigorously brushed her teeth, spitting out frequently. Then she repeated the actions, this time able to appreciate the minty flavor. She spit again, took a mouthful of water and gargled. She finished by splashing the cold water across her face.

She undressed and satisfied the temperature of the shower water would not scald her skin, she moved carefully into the stall. She shampooed her hair and, as she rinsed the suds out, she began to feel clean. She scrubbed her body with a soapy washcloth. She turned the water off and took one of the white towels to wrap around her hair. The other she took and gently dried her skin.

Although she hated to wear the clothes she had worn to the cabin, she had no choice. She put them on and left the foggy bathroom. She heard voices down the hall. Ben Williams had arrived. He and Walker were talking in low voices. Ben saw her.

"Daisy, come on over here."

Daisy was relieved to see him.

"Let's get you checked out. Medic?" he motioned to one of the EMTs who remained in the cabin.

"I'm okay. I just need to get home and I'll be all right."

Ben insisted. The technician took Daisy's vital signs and said she seemed fine. The long hot shower had done a lot to restore her.

"I'll give you a ride in a minute. Can you go wait by my car?"

Daisy obeyed and the sheriff soon joined her.

As they drove along Daisy asked, "What happened with Mrs. Walker?"

"They're taking her to the hospital. They sedated her to get her there, but she should be okay after she rests. She might need some more medicine, but that will be up to the doctors. Walker told me that she came upon Caleb in the yard, dead, and insisted that Walker put him in the small cabin where she could tend to him. She refused to believe he was dead."

CHAPTER 31

When Daisy went to the hospital the next morning, she found Retta Walker sitting erect in a straight-backed chair and gazing at the trees and houses up the hill across the street. Her long black hair had been untangled, washed, and brushed until it glistened in the morning sunlight coming through the window. Her face was clean and needed no makeup to enhance her beauty. She was not an old woman, as she had seemed in the cabin, but a woman in her fifties at the most.

"Mrs. Walker?" Daisy said.

Retta turned and said, "Please call me Retta. You're the person who found me, aren't you?"

Daisy was speechless. Instead of the wild mountain

woman who had attacked her just days earlier, there Retta Walker sat like royalty welcoming her subjects to court. The velvety crimson robe she wore completed the effect.

Daisy regained her own poise enough to say, "I'm so glad to see you like this." She could not think of anything else to say so just stood shifting her weight from one foot to another, then walked to the window to join Retta contemplating the scenery.

"Please don't blame my husband. He thought he was doing what was best for me."

Daisy nodded her head once in agreement although she was not sure she agreed. It seemed to her that the only person who had benefitted from allowing Retta to live in a state of continual madness was Walker, and she still was not convinced that his wealth came from his wife's profits from the casino in Cherokee. In a good year, the per capita distribution was around $13,000, enough to provide for only a basic lifestyle. The tribe benefitted most from employment opportunities at Harrah's or in the surrounding attractions designed to entertain and educate tourists to the area.

When Daisy told her father everything that had happened, he had provided a history of the Walkers. The family had made their fortune running stills in the early twentieth century, then by bootlegging liquor and beer when Prohibition had ended in most of the country but kept the South in its grip. Those days had long passed. Daisy was positive that Walker had found another illegal way to make money, either drugs or guns.

She imagined that Retta either did not approve of his criminal doings or was kept in an insane state so she could not notice. But why did Caleb have to die?

Daisy rolled ideas in her mind as Walker, the object of her ruminations, walked into the hospital room. She felt guilty in Retta's presence for harboring those thoughts about her husband, as if she were betraying this regal woman. She attempted to turn her attention to view of the trees that were starting to change into autumn colors.

"You look so good! Do you know when you'll leave the hospital?"

"I think I can once the doctor visits this morning. He said he'll have some prescriptions for me, too."

As Walker bent over to kiss his wife's forehead, Daisy thought she saw her cringe slightly, pulling her body away from his. Daisy believed her hunches about Walker were true, but, if they were, wouldn't Retta use this opportunity to get more help and escape?

Daisy asked, "Will you have to come back for follow-ups with the doctor?"

"I have an appointment next week," Retta answered.

Walker added, "But I'm sure she can use company, Daisy. You come visit a lot. After all, if it weren't for you, we'd still be stuck in all that craziness."

"I'd really like that. I guess I'd better go. Maybe I'll come by tomorrow to see if you need anything from town? I could call first." Daisy looked at Walker.

"Know what?" he said. "I can never remember that

number. I'll get it for you when you come by."

"Well, I'd better go and let y'all get ready to go home."

She was about to leave although she was still concerned about Retta's safety. "Is Jasmine able to come look after you?"

"Yes, but she can't get away from her job until Saturday. I haven't seen her in months so I'm very excited."

"Look, why don't you stay at my father's place until she can get here? Lucas has a nice guest room and I'm sure he wouldn't mind," Daisy addressed Retta directly.

"I'd like that, Daisy, but I'd feel better if you'd call and ask him. He could have other plans."

Daisy went outside to call her father although she knew he would welcome Retta as he would anyone Daisy asked him to put up. She wanted to ensure that Lucas would not also encourage Walker to stay at the house. She still held him as a prime suspect in the criminal activity happening around Franklin.

When she returned to them, she said, "He told me he would be disappointed if you refused his hospitality."

"I don't know how I can ever repay you, Daisy. You really don't have to do all of this."

"You know the Chinese proverb, "If you save somebody's life, you are responsible for them forever."

Whether Walker thought it was a good idea for Retta to go there or not, he was left with no option but to agree. Daisy had an answer for every objection, and Retta seemed to be looking forward to recuperating at the McLaren home.

"Great, I'll go get everything ready for you."

To Walker she said, "Do you know where my dad lives?"

Walker nodded.

"Call when you are on the way."

With that settled, Daisy left the Walkers at the hospital for the time being. When she reached the highway, she called Lexie to tell her everything that had transpired and especially about Retta's transformation.

"You wouldn't believe how beautiful she is. She was so frightening at the cabin with Caleb's body and now—I hardly know where to start. You'll have to see for yourself. Oh, and Jasmine will be here this weekend. That should be interesting. I haven't seen her since high school."

Lexie interrupted.

"About Jasmine. This morning Keira told me that she saw her at Walmart, either last week or the week before. She couldn't be sure."

CHAPTER 32

Daisy drove directly to Walgreen's. She took a basket and loaded it with soaps and bath bombs, hand and body lotions, shampoos, and conditioners. She selected a boar bristle brush and added some headbands and scrunchies for fun. Walking down the makeup aisle Daisy was perplexed. Even at Retta's age, which Daisy judged to be about fifty, her natural beauty was such that Daisy thought makeup would only detract. Her eyebrows and lashes were the same striking black as her hair. She settled on a soft rosy blush and a nude lipstick.

The Walkers were a lot younger than Daisy had thought, closer to fifty than her father's seventy plus. Jasmine must have been born when Retta was barely out of her teens. No wonder that she couldn't control Jasmine. Daisy remembered Jasmine as running with a wild crowd at Franklin High. With the group that would get one member of the group, who was already old enough or who had a fake ID, to buy beer. They would drive out in the country, sometimes on the banks of the Little Tennessee River, to party most of the night.

Daisy's class had a few rebels in it, but most of the teens her age preferred sports and hiking in the mountains rather than partying all night. They would meet at the library to gossip and study together on weeknights. Weekends they would meet in couples or in groups for activities. Jake and Daisy usually paired off to hike the old trails.

As she paid, she grabbed a few of the magazines on racks below the check-out counter. She selected a couple containing gossip about celebrities and several with recipes. News could wait until Retta was stronger.

In the car Daisy rang up Lucas's office. Maxie answered the phone. "Hi, Daisy."

"May I speak to my dad?"

"He's in a closing. What's up?"

"Did he tell you about Caleb Walker? And Retta?"

"He did. He was pretty angry that you went up there alone, after he got over being relieved. Don't ever do anything like that again."

"I promise." Daisy eagerly changed the subject. "Can you let him know that Retta accepted our invitation? She'll be there this afternoon. I'm going now to get everything ready for her."

"He was going home right after the closing, but he should call in, so I'll tell him."

CHAPTER 33

The petite stray cat was peering through the spindles of the staircase to Daisy's apartment over the garage. The cat stuck her head out, and Daisy reached to pet her.

"Have you been waiting here all morning?" Daisy said. "No? You heard the car?" Daisy used the kindly high-pitched voice people assumed when speaking to a small cat or dog. The calico was growing on her.

Now ignoring Daisy, the cat turned and with straight-up tail padded up the stairs. Daisy followed and went directly to her bedroom to deposit her things on the bed. When she returned to the great room, the cat was sitting on the small round table and was busy cleaning her paws. Daisy watched for a minute as the cat spread her claws out and licked between each toe. When she found something disagreeable, she gnawed at it. Daisy shook her head, left the cat on the table, put fresh water in the water bowl, and grabbed a Coke for herself.

She returned to her bedroom and moved her laptop to the small desk under a window. She retrieved the book she had purchased along with one given to her by Lucas, to read about the Spanish exploration of North Carolina mountains in the 1500s. That afternoon she and Jake would film the feature report on the legend of de Soto at the Nikwasi Mound in Franklin, and she had slacked off on her research. She set the books on the table as she fixed a cup of coffee.

Taking the book written by Margaret Siler and the coffee to the couch, Daisy settled in to see what the earliest accounts reported. Siler's book, published in the 1930s, was the most recent of the writings Daisy had found. She claimed she had dug a cannonball left by de Soto's army out of a field on a farm along with a small, abandoned cannon which she claimed was buried near that same farm. According to Siler, de Soto had led his army through the Cullasaja Gap to the route to the Ohio Valley. Daisy, who dreaded the drive through the gap to Highlands, wondered at that. She tried to imagine and army with horses and cannons attempting this trek.

She was also curious about the passage describing the princess's robes which were inset with precious gems, a necklace of pearls, and the ruby ring given to her by de Soto. She wore a ring that looked to de Soto like gold.

She was about to read about the path the Spaniards took through the mountains when suddenly the cat jumped off the table and darted to the front door. A few seconds later there was a knock. Looking out of a window, Daisy was surprised to see Nathan Stark. She opened the door and invited him in. She remained just inside the door, so he did not try to go farther into the room. They both stood by the door. The cat abandoned them and sauntered into the bedroom.

"How are you doing? You had quite a shock at the Walker place."

"I'm doing all right. I'm glad Retta is getting the help she needs. Do you know yet how Caleb died?"

"Off the record. Caleb had been shot. His father heard the shot, went out, and found Caleb outside the old cabin. He carried his body and laid it on the bed. The mother insisted that he leave it there."

"That's awful," Daisy exclaimed. "Was it an accident? Why would anyone shoot Caleb?"

"Off the record. We're pretty certain that Caleb was part of a group of drug smugglers, the people who have been bringing opiates and meth from Atlanta. That's why I'm here. I heard you said you saw a man running away from the plane crash."

"That's right. He was running downhill from the crash."

"Can you describe what he looked like?"

"I only saw him for a few seconds before he disappeared into the forest, but he looked like he could be from here. He had long hair and a beard. A ponytail.

Wore a checked shirt like the flannel shirts that are common around here. Green and black. You can buy them at Walmart."

"You didn't know him?"

"No, he looked like half the men in Franklin. Sorry."

"Was he carrying anything?"

"I don't think so," Daisy paused. "I really couldn't tell."

"I don't want to alarm you unnecessarily, but don't write about the man or tell anyone outside of your family and the sheriff. If he thinks you could identify him, you'll be in danger. I think some of these gang members may have killed Caleb."

"I've already told my father and Jake."

"Please tell them not to spread this around. All of you could already be in danger."

"Jake'll be here soon. We are working on a story this afternoon."

"Here's my card. Call me if you think you are in danger or if you remember anything else about the crash."

Nathan turned to leave but Daisy touched his arm to stop him.

"Have you heard anything that suggests treasure hunting or jewels could be involved?"

He raised his eyebrows to give a quizzical look.

"I mean, I've been reading some historical accounts of the county, and they refer to treasures consisting of pearls, rubies, and other precious gems that could still be located here. Either buried or hidden some other way."

Nathan shook his head.

"No. We're only investigating drug smuggling. Why?"

"Well, it's just that I was doing some research for the film that Jake and I are making about de Soto, the Spanish explorer. Whether he passed through Franklin with a Native American princess, or not. I came across descriptions of precious jewels and pearls that might have gone missing. They'd be worth a fortune today if someone found them."

"I'm not aware of anything involving jewelry thefts."

"Sure. Sorry I bothered you."

Nathan looked calmly into Daisy's eyes. "No problem. I don't think you'd ever be able to bother me."

Daisy wondered what he could have meant by that last statement. As soon as he left, Daisy locked up her apartment and went to her father's house. She put the toiletries and some fresh towels in the room where Retta would stay. She called Ed to let him know Retta would convalesce at Lucas's.

As she finished with the preparations, Jake arrived, and they set out to film the story about the Cherokee and de Soto at the Nikwasi Mound.

CHAPTER 34

I've been reading a lot about the Cherokees and Spanish explorers in the Smoky Mountains. Margaret Siler seemed certain that de Soto brought Chualiah, as she called the princess, to Franklin, and that she was rescued when braves who had followed along attacked the party on the Little Tennessee close to the mound."

"You have been busy," Jake said.

"And from what I read in James Mooney's account from sources recounting Cherokee legends, it's possible that de Soto did come to Franklin. It was recorded that he sent scouts who went as far south from the Asheville area as Franklin.

"They would've reported back to him that they'd

found a working farm community where the army could stock up on corn and other supplies. Remember, an army travels on its stomach,"

"Have they found any physical evidence of the Spanish here?"

"Siler says a Spanish cannonball was found in a field north of town. But one of the most interesting facts which the accounts mentioned was a treasure of pearls and precious stones that seem to have disappeared. Also, although it was written that the Native American queen or princess escaped and returned to her home, there is no record of her actually reaching Cofitachiqui, the town she came from."

"Darlin', I take it you think that treasure is still in Franklin."

"Well, it could be. It has to be somewhere."

"If it ever existed."

Daisy was prepared to continue the argument until she won, but they reached the Nikwasi Mound and Jake parked.

Nikwasi Mound was unimpressive from a distance. To those driving by and not bothering to stop, it looked small and unkempt. Patches of weeds littered the surface. Crowded over the years by paved roads, warehouses, and strip malls, the mound was fortunate that it had not been razed for a parking lot.

The Eastern Band of the Cherokee and concerned citizens of Franklin who were interested in preserving the site fought until it was returned by the town to the Eastern Band. A plaque describing its importance in

Cherokee history had been installed. It read, "NIKWASI: This mound marks site of old Cherokee town, Nikwasi. A council of Sir Alexander Cuming with the Indians here led to a treaty, 1730."

The mound stood humbly at one end of a one-story warehouse row. The warehouses once stored supplies transported overland. Lucas had been a prominent member of a group that traveled to Atlanta to get a railroad trunk line constructed, with trains to carry passengers. That movement got as far as a feasibility study and died when the study showed that visitors to the North Carolina mountains preferred Highlands and Asheville, that the primary tourists in Franklin were retirees come to spend a few days looking for treasure in the mountain streams. It resulted in the transformation of the Georgia Highway from a two-lane to four, however, the wealthiest tourists still made the jaunt to Highlands for the cool summers.

Lucas's group then turned its attention to rehabilitating the area and had an impressive brick post office constructed, but that was it. Interest in Depot Street died out, and the remaining depots were turned into auto repair shops, used car dealerships and other mom and pop businesses.

The Nikwasi Mound looked even more bedraggled up close, but its size was more impressive. Daisy was dwarfed as she stood beside it. Jake started to film from a distance and moved in slowly until he was a few yards away, and the mound towered above her.

"We drive past it every day. Often, we aren't even

aware of its presence, but the Nikwasi Mound has watched over Franklin since the days our town was known as the center of activity for Native Americans in the valley. The mound was constructed over a thousand years ago, possibly as a ceremonial house. Whether it was a dwelling for spirits or for a ruler or priest we may never know. One thing we do know is that it still holds its mysteries close."

Daisy continued her narrative, adding details about the Cherokee Nation in the Smokies. She recounted the legend of de Soto and the Cherokee queen. To finish she said, "Will we ever know where Chualiah ended her days? Will the lost treasure box of jewels and pearls ever be found? We may never know because, as I said before, the Nikwasi Mound holds tight its centuries-old mysteries."

When they had completed the story, they went next door to have lunch at a new restaurant and to talk about their plans for the evening.

"Are we still going to the Ruby?" Jake said, referring to the theater showing the latest Bond movie.

"Sure. Lexie told me they'll meet us there. We can have dinner with Lucas beforehand." Daisy shifted in her chair. "Retta Walker is going to stay until she is stronger."

"Daisy! Their son was just murdered, and no one knows why. Why on earth would you want her to stay at Lucas's? You're just asking for trouble. Can't you ever just let things be?"

"That's exactly why she needs to be at Daddy's.

Whoever killed Caleb could go back and hurt her!"

"But that's not your problem, Daisy." Jake crumpled his napkin and flung it and the silverware on the plate. "That's for Ben to do, or the FBI."

Snatching her plate and glass, Daisy stood up. "You're impossible, Jacob Smith. Besides, what's done is done. Walker is bringing her over this afternoon."

"I hope he's not staying there too.

"I've got to meet Walker and Retta." Daisy left the table abruptly.

"Is Walker staying too? Daisy?"

"No, Jake, Walker has not been invited to stay. Just Retta. Happy now?"

Jake followed her toward the door. They dropped off their plates at the counter and went outside together.

"I know you're afraid I might get hurt, too, but look—Daddy and Ed will be there for the weekend. You can come over and stay, too, if that would make you feel better. You can make sure Walker doesn't try to horn in and sleep over."

"I'll be there right after work."

CHAPTER 35

Lucas's car was in the driveway, so Daisy pulled up beside it and joined them in the kitchen. Ed had put one of his specialties, a big pan of lasagna, in the oven. Rather than using the traditional ragu layers, he alternated the pasta with his creamy Bolognese sauce and a Bechamel.

"Will you need extra Parmesan?" Daisy started grating the chunk of cheese with a fine grater.

"Yeah, never hurts. Why don't you make a salad dressing?"

The Walkers arrived. Walker carried Retta's suitcase. "I'll take that. Retta, let me show you where you'll stay." Daisy rolled the luggage to the guest room and placed it on the bed. Retta followed close behind.

Daisy took the towels from the bed to the attached bathroom and retuned with a Walgreen's bag.

"I bought some things for you." She picked up the bag and emptied the contents onto the bed. "Let me know if you need anything else."

"This is perfect, Daisy. I can't thank you enough. Seeing Caleb like that...."

Daisy did not know what to say.

"Walker did what he thought best for me. He thought time would heal my grief. He got some antidepressants for me that helped, but it destroyed me, seeing my baby like that. It still seems like a dream. I can't believe he's gone."

"I'm so sorry Retta. Remember, Jasmine will be here soon. Maybe she can stay a while to help you and Walker."

Retta slumped on the bed. "Oh, Jasmine. The mountain's no place for her. I tried to send her away when she was young. The boys around here were getting wild, and you know what her dad was doing. The bootlegging. So he was no help. I didn't want her to get caught up in a wild crowd, or to get hurt, so I wanted to send her to board at the school at Rabun Gap, but she would have none of that. When Jasmine doesn't agree, you might as well give up at the get go.

"She's in Atlanta now and it takes something like this to get her to visit. She comes home for some holidays, but she's usually too busy with work."

"Come and get it while it's hot," Ed bellowed, and the two women returned to the kitchen.

Lasagna and salad were already on the large table.

"You can get your own sweet tea or regular, or water, at the counter." Ed grabbed two sweet teas and sat by Lucas. "Mr. Walker, can you bring that basket of bread?"

Walker got it and sat next to Retta.

"It's good to have y'all here with us tonight," Lucas began after everyone was seated. "Retta, you've been through quite an ordeal. I spoke with the doctors at the hospital, and they told me you are in remarkably good health when you take that into consideration.

"I hope you will make yourself at home here. Stay long as you need to, and certainly stay until we know how and why Caleb died. We want you to feel safe. Perhaps as you continue to recover, you'll come to remember some of what has been happening to your family, and Walker, you come visit whenever you can or stay over if you need to. Now let's eat this good meal Ed and Daisy have made."

With impeccable timing Jake walked on to the scene. He nodded greetings to everyone. "Lucas. Daisy," he singled out.

Daisy explained, "Jake and I are going to see the new Bond movie at the Ruby with Lexie and Brad."

"Have you eaten?" Ed asked. "Help yourself. There's sweet tea, too."

"I remember the first James Bond movie I ever saw," Lucas said. "Goldfinger. With your mother. We were just kids. Sophomores in high school, I think, and I had just started asking her out.

"That might have been the first date we ever went on. She would grab hold of me and hide her eyes on my shoulder when she got scared." Lucas chuckled. "I think she was pretending though, to have an excuse to hug me.

"I didn't have money for popcorn and Cokes. Barely had enough for the tickets."

The room was clouded in a hush.

"Daisy looks a lot like her, doesn't she?" Jake asked.

"Yes, the spitting image."

Lucas changed the subject of conversation. "Is Jasmine able to come see you?"

"She's supposed to get here tomorrow. Late. Then she'll have to get back to work by Monday."

"You know, Retta, I used to think Jasmine and Caleb were twins. Until they went to school. Caleb was big for his age, wasn't he?"

"That's right, and Jasmine was so petite. I worried so much about her because she was so small. Turns out I didn't need to at all."

When they had finished eating, Daisy walked Walker to his truck.

"In all of the confusion I wasn't able to ask you how long Caleb's body had been lying there."

"It was upsetting all right. I'm sorry you had to go through that," he looked askance at Daisy. "I'm really glad you're OK."

Daisy turned to face him as he was opening the door of the truck. "So, how long had Caleb been dead? Do you have any idea who killed him?"

"No, I don't know who killed him! Don't you think I would've said?"

"The way you let him stay there after you knew Retta was going to him—I'm not sure. So, how long was he there?"

"Well. I don't rightly know. Let's see, I followed Retta there about four days ago so maybe a week?"

Daisy opened her mouth to ask why he was giving her a different account from the story he had told Nathan but thought better of it. Her gut was telling her that Walker was hedging and that he was very practiced at avoiding the truth. Unfortunately, her gut was no help in figuring out how or even if Retta was involved in the events that followed the plane crash.

CHAPTER 36

The gravel parking lot at the Ruby Cinema was almost full. Daisy and Jake saw Maxie with her date on the way in. Maxie was glowing. The ruby pendant was her only jewelry. Her emerald-green midi dress fitted her perfectly and enhanced rather than emphasized her curves. Beaming she waved at Daisy.

"Hey there," Maxie said. "Y'all know David Tenant. He works at the Walmart pharmacy."

"Sure," Daisy said. "Hi David."

She realized that she had never paid him much attention at the pharmacy. Wearing his white lab coat and always busy at his counter in front of the stacks filled with prescription medications, he blended into his surroundings. Now as he wore a sport coat and dark blue jeans, she could see what Maxie saw in him.

The couples exchanged pleasantries and headed inside. "I heard you met with Nathan. How'd that go?" Maxie asked.

Jake looked inquiringly at Daisy. "You saw Nathan Stark? When was that?"

Daisy ignored Jake's questions and looked at Maxie.

"He wanted to learn what I saw at the plane crash. That was all."

"Why were you meeting with Nathan Stark?" Jake asked.

Daisy took Maxie's arm and walked ahead with her, leaving Jake in David Tenant's company. Jake gave up.

Maxie said, "Did Nathan tell you that the plane was carrying a shipment of drugs? The pilot was high as a kite! He was on an FBI watch list." As usual, Maxie was Daisy's best source for all news regarding criminals.

Daisy just raised her eyebrows, cocked her head, and shook it at Maxie.

"Later," Daisy said to Maxie.

"Did he say that?" Jake had a hurt tone in his voice.

Lexie and Brad joined them, and once again Daisy was relieved to have an excuse not to answer Jake's repeated questions.

"I heard you rescued Lexie the other day," Brad said.

"Sure did. Where were you?"

"Just hanging out downtown."

Daisy could not see Brad doing anything that

sounded so frivolous. When she was in Chapel Hill, hanging out meant that she and her friends spent a lot of time sitting together on the grass on McCorkle Place or in the patio at He's Not Here, a favorite local bar. Often, even when studying in the library, they would take breaks to either sit on one of the low walls or to grab a snack in the Student Union.

However, Brad was definitely not a hanger-outer type of man. Whatever he had been doing, he clearly did not want to share with Daisy. Daisy knew him well enough not to pursue the matter. She assumed it was work-related for Brad and he would never spill information about his work. Lexie and Brad had only shared Brad's involvement with security services because they regarded her as one of their closest friends in Franklin. They knew she would never betray their trust.

The theater was packed with people excited about the latest 007 movie, and Daisy and Jake could not get their usual aisle seats. They had to sit close to the screen and kept their heads tilted up for the entire movie.

"Were you planning to tell me about seeing Nathan Stark?" Jake asked.

"Look, Jake, he came by the house to ask me about the crash. That's all. It was a professional visit. There was really nothing to tell."

She took Jake's hand and squeezed it. It was not like Jake to be jealous so perhaps he was simply worried about her. If she broke Nathan's confidentiality, Jake would only have more reasons to fret so she kept silent. If he were jealous of Nathan, Daisy did not know what to think.

After the movie they all ended the evening at the Lazy Hiker Brewing Company for drinking a craft beer and dancing to music provided by a DJ. When the band took a break, Daisy snagged a seat by David.

"Your work must be pretty interesting?" Daisy began.

"I wouldn't think pharmacy would interest most people," David said, "unless you find talking with people about aches and pains, real and imagined, interesting. It's mainly about precision when measuring, and of course you have to become proficient at reading doctors' handwriting."

"But you have an opportunity to really help people, for example, Joe Taylor," Daisy, not to be deterred, forged ahead. "I understand he had an addiction problem for several years. Had he gotten help for that?"

"Are you asking if he was ever on methadone?" David replied. "That's not something I'd know about. It would have been handled at the recovery clinic out Old Wayah Road, but I don't think they will tell you anything about Joe. They strictly guard their patients' privacy."

Jake took Daisy's hand and pulled her up. "Let's dance. They're playing our song."

The repetitive opening chords of "Let's Do It" were calling a crowd to the dance floor.

"You don't even like the Black-Eyed Peas, Jake."

"And I don't think David even liked being grilled about Joe Taylor. So we're even."

Jake led Daisy outside to the patio. A line had formed at the food truck.

"Are you hungry?"

"No, I'm not hungry, and I want to go back inside."

"Look Daisy, the man is on a date. Your good friend Maxie is on a date. Do you really think they want you butting in on their date?"

Daisy had no quick answer to those questions. Lacking a sassy retort, she said nothing at first.

"I think Joe Taylor was murdered."

"Daisy, stop it."

"I don't mean that somebody planned to murder him and did it with heroin. What I mean is that I believe the heroin was brought to Franklin on that plane. Whoever sold it didn't cut it to reduce the strength. Joe was unlucky. Probably his first time to try it. Whoever was with him was lucky they didn't go first.

"I think that might have been Keira, and I'm going to try to ask her about it."

Jake shook his head, took Daisy by the shoulders, and looked her in the eye.

"I'm really worried that you are getting in over your head. I'm afraid of what could happen to you, Daisy."

CHAPTER 37

The cat's eyes shone a phosphorescent green in the glare of the headlights as Jake stopped his truck beside the stairs to Daisy's apartment over the garage.

"How did she get outside?"

Daisy climbed out of the truck's cab. The cat rushed over and circled between her legs, then yowled and streaked up to the stairs ahead of Daisy.

Jake got out of the car and said, "Wait, Daisy, are you sure you left it in your apartment?"

Daisy had reached her front door and was fixing to unlock it. She stopped and looked down at Jake.

"I meant to put her out so she wouldn't make a mess. When I'd left, I realized that after hearing about drugs from Nathan I had forgotten. I'm positive."

"Hold on a minute then." Jake climbed the stairs. "Give me your keys."

Daisy did not argue with him this time. He turned the key and opened the do. The cat zoomed in ahead of them both, ran over to her bowls, and lapped up some water.

"Wait here," Jake said. Cautiously he entered her bedroom. He checked the small bathroom and her closet. He went back to the great room. "Come on in. No one here now."

Daisy stepped in and studied the room. "It looks all right. Maybe Ed came to borrow something. I can check with him tomorrow."

"Look in your room."

Her bedroom looked the same. Propped against a pillow the stray cat was now sitting on her haunches cleaning her private parts. "Back to normal, I guess." Daisy turned to return to the great room when she stopped.

"My laptop!"

Jake glanced at the small table where the laptop rested open. "It's there. What about it?"

"I always log out and close it before leaving."

"Maybe you forgot?"

"I never ever forget to do that. It's an extra procedure to keep hackers out."

"I'm convinced. Pack a bag and grab the cat, too, if you want. I'm taking you to Lucas's for the night."

"I won't be run out of my own home." Daisy stood

her ground. "I'm getting ready for bed."

"If that's the case, I'm taking the couch."

"Suit yourself," Daisy said as she threw the other pillow at him, shooed him out, and slammed the door to her room. "I'm going to sleep."

She washed her face and brushed her teeth. Shoving the stray off her own spot she propped up in bed to read more of Mooney's book.

She turned to the description of de Soto crossing a high mountain range and then descending to a stream flowing north. Mooney assumed he had reached the French Broad River at Asheville, but Daisy thought the description as a "stream" better fit the Little Tennessee at Franklin.

If de Soto arrived in Franklin rather than Asheville and headed west, then Peachtree, North Carolina, could be the "Guaxule" referred to in Mooney.

She let that thought go for the moment and turned her attention to the infamous Trail of Tears, euphemistically referred to as The Removal. General Winfield Scott ordered the Cherokee who had not voluntarily left their homes and land to relocate in Oklahoma to be rounded up and held in previously-built stockades until they could be transferred to a point near Cleveland, Tennessee.

In the harsh winter of 1838, they were forced to walk across the country to the new Indian Territory in Oklahoma. Many died waiting for a break in the ice floes which frequently blocked the Mississippi River. Those able to continue the march died from disease, starvation, and continued exposure to the extreme cold. Daisy shivered as she thought of the Cherokee men, women, and children who suffered and died along the way.

Many of her friends had some degree of Cherokee blood and had been told the traditional stories of how their grandparents, aunts, and uncles were removed from their farms and villages because of new settlers coveted their rich farmlands. The discovery of gold on Cherokee land created an influx of prospectors eager to lay claim on native-owned properties.

They told her of the legend Tsali, Charley. Tsali's family had been taken by force and were mistreated by the soldiers. When they kept prodding his wife with their bayonets, Tsali spoke in Cherokee and told his tribesmen to attack the troops. He surrendered himself and his sons for execution so the rest of his tribe could remain on their properties.

Daisy had seen the legend portrayed in the outdoor drama *Unto These Hills* at the Qualla Boundary in Cherokee. She had always been moved by the long history of oppression since de Soto first came in search of gold and treasures. Restitution had been made by the United States in 1905, totaling $1,000,000. When divided among the 30,000 eligible, the figure came to $33 per person. More recent payments by the federal government attempted to grant an equitable settlement, but to Daisy's way of thinking the payments held more of a symbolic value, a recognition that a great wrong had been done. No amount of money could ever restore the tribal integrity of the Cherokee people.

As she fell asleep, Daisy realized that, accompanied by Jake and the cat, she had not had a panic attack.

CHAPTER 38

Jake had already left by the time Daisy awoke the next morning.

"Thank God," Daisy said aloud as she made a Keurig and popped a bagel in the wide-slot toaster. She replenished the cat's bowls with water and tuna from an aluminum packet of lemon-pepper spiced tuna. "I hope that suits you. I'll get some regular cat food later today."

The cat looked up and seemed to shrug as if to say, "I'll believe it when I see it." It daintily lapped its water.

Daisy ate her bagel in front of the television. It was Saturday and the local news had come and gone. Daisy was unconcerned that she had missed it as the plane crash was already old news. She had not seen any of the reports she and Jake had sent, but that was all right with her as well. Living through it was enough for her. Daisy flipped to the Weather Channel. The local forecasts scrolled fast along the bottom of the screen. At last, Franklin, clear until Monday when another tropical storm would arrive.

With the cat secured in the apartment, Daisy stepped out to a glorious morning. Bright sun belied the horror of the previous week. She breathed in the fresh air. Jake's truck was not there.

When she entered the kitchen of the big house, Lucas was alone reading the newspaper at the table. He had eaten breakfast, and Ed had already cleaned up and gone out for the day.

"Want more coffee?' Daisy asked.

"Sure."

"You know, I've been wanting to talk with you? I'm glad I've caught you alone."

Lucas set aside the paper.

"Talk? What about? Are you okay?"

Daisy crossed the room slowly with the two coffees and set one, just the way he liked it, in front of Lucas.

"I drove out to the road where Mom died."

"Not by yourself, I hope."

"Dad," Daisy lowered her head to caution him to stop. "I was trying to find out if there were any other reason for another person to be in those woods. Or if there were tangible evidence that another person had been there; I didn't find any."

"I see," Lucas said gently. "So how can I help?"

Daisy, wanting to know but fearing the answer to

her question, gazed into space and stirred her coffee. What if her mother were meeting someone, a man? What if her parents' marriage were not as perfect as it had seemed?

"I know you told me that Mom died in a car accident, and I can accept that, I guess."

Daisy looked Lucas in the eyes.

"But what I have never known is why she was on that road to begin with." She struggled to find the words to ask what she needed to know. "Was she meeting someone? Were you and Mom getting along?"

Daisy sobbed, "I really need to know—whatever it is."

Lucas reached his arms toward her. "Of course, sweetie. Come here. It's not that bad."

She hugged him tightly and gradually her weeping ceased.

"Come now," Lucas said. Have a seat and drink your coffee, and I'll tell you the whole story."

"Where should I begin? Do you remember how your mother and I met?"

"Of course. You were both at UNC. You were studying law and Mom, social work."

"That's right. She stopped working when you were born, but then, when you went away to Carolina, she got a job with the Macon County Department of Social Services."

Daisy interrupted, "She was really excited to get back to work. She planned to save up so she and I could do a Grand Tour of Europe when I graduated."

"That she did," Lucas said. "I think she would've wished you'd do that now on your own—but that's neither here nor there."

"She worked in the Child Protective Services division. She had to investigate some awful situations. Neglect, abuse, you probably went to school with older brothers and sisters of some of the children she had to look after."

Daisy interrupted once again, "You know she took me with her one time. To a house. She had to pick up one of the cheerleaders from Franklin High and take her to a safe house. Mom thought my presence would be reassuring to her—Amy. I just remembered her as a little kid." Daisy shook her head. "Amy had confided in her pastor who convinced her to contact social services."

"Your mother was able to help her though high school, and now she's at WCU in Cullowhee."

"Mom was so good at her job."

Lucas got up using his cane to get more coffee. "Let me, Daddy."

"No, no," he said. "The doctor wants me to try to do more for myself. The walker is so I won't overtax myself."

Seated again with a fresh cup, Lucas resumed his narrative.

"One day she got a call from a social worker in Cherokee. A report came in from Franklin that a young girl had been forcibly abducted from a community just north of here. The girl was 17, and your mother spoke with several people in the small town to make sure she had not run away. Hoping to find more opportunities, kids often leave on their own to go to Asheville or Atlanta."

"She found two reliable witnesses to the kidnapping who had heard the girl's screams. As Alice continued to investigate, she learned of other girls who were thought to have run away, but who had never been heard from again. She contacted social services in Atlanta and Asheville for help in tracking them down."

"Were they able to do that?" Daisy asked.

"As Alice thought, a good number of the girls ended up in need of help. Several decided to return to Franklin, but most stayed away and got food stamps and other aid."

"So, none were kidnapped?" Daisy bowed her head in thought.

"I didn't say that. In both Atlanta and Asheville almost 30 per cent of the girls remained unaccounted for. Eight girls in all—nine when we include another girl we know was abducted but was found. Not one of the eight have ever returned to their homes, and no one knows what became of them."

"That's terrible, Dad."

"That it is, Daisy! I guess you can see why I might be a little overprotective of you at times."

"A little?" Daisy and Lucas laughed together. Then Daisy's face turned dark again.

"And Mom was trying to find those girls?"

"Not at first," Lucas said. "Ali and I discussed the situation many times and decided there were too many possibilities. They could have been swallowed up in Atlanta or Asheville or moved on to another city. The girls hadn't been killed; unidentified bodies were routinely cross-checked in social services department records."

"There were simply too many things that might have happened, and the Social Services Division had, and still has, limited resources. Girls continued to disappear, and she would investigate, but she had too many people, like Amy, needing her help."

"I see," Daisy said, "but I still don't understand what this has to do with Mom's accident."

"I'm getting to that. It was early spring. You had gone to Emerald Isle for your last Spring Break. It was mid-April and still very cool here. The trees were beginning to bud out, dappling the woods with soft greens. The dogwoods and redbuds were beginning to blossom. Ali and I were very excited about your upcoming graduation. I had booked a room at the Carolina Inn well in advance. Alice had bought a lovely dress for the occasion. Things had never been better, and yes, we were still very much in love.

"Then one morning, when I was at the office, she got a call. It was an anonymous tip about a cabin deep in the woods that was being used as a brothel. She told me and I advised her to contact the sheriff and police and to let them handle it. She said that she would."

"That was the last time I ever spoke with her."

"Oh, Daddy," Daisy clung to her father and broke down. Tears flowed but she could make no sound. No cry could express the depth of the sorrow she felt for her father, and her own grief seemed far away. The two, father and daughter, sat motionless.

"You are so much like your mother."

Daisy roused herself and went to the bathroom. As she looked at herself in the mirror, for a moment, she saw her mother's face. She dried her tears, washed her face, and returned to Lucas.

"Daddy, I'm so sorry I put you through this. If I had known how painful it would be...."

"It's okay, sweetie. You deserve the truth. We both need to move on, to get on with life."

CHAPTER 39

Daisy reached her Jeep and got in the driver's seat before breaking down. Plagued with fears about her mother's last moments, she unleashed a torrent of tears she had dammed up for years. Her mother had been murdered because of something she discovered on that mountain. Daisy considered her next move. Whatever had happened to her mother, she was more certain than ever that Mr. Walker was involved.

She drove to the place where her mother had died and, after getting her bearings, set off in the direction of the Walkers' farm. When she reached a stream that she knew ran along Ruby Mine Road to the Simpson mine, she searched for a place to cross. She walked down to a spot where no laurel or brambles hugged the banks. There was a rocky overhang she could balance herself on once she leapt across. That was the moment she saw a body under the overhang.

Daisy stifled a scream. She looked around to see if anyone was coming after her before continuing to cross the stream. Using her walking stick as a pole, she vaulted across to the small cave.

She did not recognize him at first glance and assumed it was the second person from the plane crash. Wearing dressy khakis and a Polo shirt, he appeared to be a city dweller—from Atlanta, Asheville, or maybe Raleigh. Increasingly, wealthy people from cities were purchasing mountain "estates" as getaways to be used by their families during summer and the winter holidays. Many flew on private planes and landed at the airport north of town. That still did not explain why this craft had been flying so low over the ridge in the opposite direction from the airport.

From the way the body was awkwardly curled into the cave, she figured someone had killed him and then dragged and pushed his body into the rocks. Squatting, she used her stick to turn him over. They had blasted him close with a shotgun and then fired a single shot into his forehead. He sprawled before her, his bloated face discolored and covered with maggots, his dried blood attracting a swarm of ants that had scattered when she moved the corpse, a gruesome sight which Daisy was unaccustomed to seeing.

Gagging, Daisy turned away. Her breath was quickening, becoming shallow, and her heart pounded against her chest. A cold sweat washed over her body. Trembling, she searched for a way out, but her feet seemed glued to the spot. She believed that if she did not regain her self-control soon, she would faint. She forced herself to breathe deeply and slowly, as she had been taught. Simultaneously, she told herself to calm down, that she was okay. When she was breathing normally, she tried her cellphone but got no signal.

She turned to see the crash site not too far off. Anxious about the noises she had heard in the woods, she decided to angle down the mountain to reach the ruby mine. She felt she would be safe there and she could call the sheriff, and maybe Jake, once there.

Exhausted from effort and emotion, she crept down the mountainside. The laurel grew thicker. Dense stands of pines had saplings growing underneath. She reached another stream that she knew led to the Simpson mine. Excited to be so close, she walked faster, staying close to the water. With the mine office in site, she slipped on a damp, moss-covered stone.

As she fell, she heard a rifle shot, then another. Too frightened to be cautious, she jumped up and ran as fast as she could to the mine. She zigzagged between the laurels while leaping over blackberry brambles and boulders, screaming for help. Her rapidly beating heart boomed in her ears and for a moment Daisy heard the familiar rhythm of a Cherokee war dance. Briars caught her skin and clothes, but even as they ripped at her she continued to flee.

A tourist couple paused with sifters in hand and stared wide-eyed at the crazed lady rushing towards them. Daisy raced past them into the two-story office building.

"Someone is trying to kill me. Call the sheriff."

Louisa seemed shocked but compliant, and she called the sheriff's office. "Is Ben there? There's been a shooting out here? Who was it…well, Daisy McLaren."

"Maxie's getting in touch with him."

Daisy's heart pounded. She sat on a bench and bent over to catch her breath. She thought about telling Louisa about the body she had stumbled upon but thought better of it. Although Daisy suspected the Walkers of being involved in any criminal activity on the mountain, it also seemed to follow that the Simpsons could be a part of it. Caleb and the Simpsons' three boys had grown up hunting in the woods and fishing in the mountain's cold streams together.

Once calm, she took out her cell and called Jake. "What do you mean? Who is shooting at you? Where are you?"

Jake had not yelled at her like that in a long time, so she hesitated, but then told him what had happened. "I was just planning to look around the crash site to see if I could find traces of a passenger who might've gotten away. It made little sense that a charter pilot would fly solo around there. And then…. There's more, but I need to tell you about it in person." She glanced at Louisa. She definitely did not feel that she could trust her, and the last thing Daisy wanted to do was to alert anyone who lived on the mountain, especially the murderer that she had discovered a body.

Well, I guess you found him, didn't you? I would've gone with you. You know that?!?"

"Yes, but you would've fussed at me too much."

Jake was silenced.

"Will you come get me? Please?"

"Of course. Leaving right now."

All was quiet in the mine office. The couple, who had been sifting for rubies, were freaked out by Daisy's sudden and alarming appearance, and had left in a hurry. Louisa was now staring at Daisy. "Law, Daisy, you look a sight! Do you need anything?"

"Your ladies' room, I guess."

She took the key. Daisy switched on the light in the room, which only had enough space for one toilet, a sink, and a trash can. It was small but clean, kept that way for the tourists who supported the business. Daisy splashed water on her face, then took a paper towel, dampened it, and rubbed around her face and neck. She ran her fingers through her short hair. She tucked her shirt back into her jeans. Feeling a little more presentable, she rejoined Louisa in the shop to wait for Jake.

Now able to think more rationally and collect her thoughts, Daisy wondered about the identity of the man whose body she had found in the overhang. The best result would be if his fingerprints were on file with the FBI, but, given the condition of the body, she was not sure that the prints could even be recovered.

CHAPTER 40

Louisa was already at the counter when Daisy came back to the shop. I wonder where she sleeps, Daisy thought. She could not imagine her walking to an upstairs bedroom as large as she was. She had the smooth, unlined face that heavy people often have. She wore an unflattering cotton print dress, no sweater, despite the autumn morning's chill. Motioning to a high stool at the counter, she pushed forward a steaming mug of coffee.

"This should warm you up. Sheriff'll be here soon."

"Thanks." Daisy gazed into the mug and hoped she could divine the reason for the attack on her and the corpse she had discovered in the forest. She had no choice but to seek refuge at the ruby mine even though she wondered whether the Simpsons could be involved in both. The mine could easily be a front to sell either illegal firearms or drugs; but, if that were the case, the simple thing would be to kill her as well and dispose of her body deep in the woods.

"Who d'you think was after you?"

Daisy studied Louisa's face to see if she was dissembling but saw only innocence and concern. She shrugged.

Jake and the sheriff drove up at the same time. Daisy was beginning to regret calling Jake. He was sure to fuss at her and maybe she deserved to be chastised. She determined to be strong and to point out that the body would likely never have been discovered had she not gone out to investigate the crash again.

When Jake rushed into the room, she dissolved into tears. Instead of shouting, he embraced her and let her weep. He stroked her head gently and said, "Now, now, darlin'. It's not as bad as you think. You're safe. I won't let anything happen to you."

Ben came in, glanced at them, and asked Louisa, "What happened?"

"Ain't sure. Daisy came flying in here like a bat out of hell and told me some'uns trying to kill her."

"Did you see anyone else? Hear anything?"

"Didn't see nothing. Heard a few shots but figured it was hunters."

Ben glanced at Daisy and Jake and nodded, "Y'all go on. I'll catch up with you later."

Jake escorted Daisy to his truck. He took off his

jacket and, after fastening her seat belt, covered her.

When they reached her home, he asked, "Do you want to go to your place or Lucas's?"

"Dad's."

Lucas was out, but, as usual, there was a pot of hot coffee warming on the Mr. Coffee. Jake settled Daisy on the sofa with a mug and went outside to call Lucas. When he returned, he said, "Do you feel like talking?"

"You were right, Jake. I should've left well enough alone." She sobbed. "I thought I was going to die. I found a dead body up there. And then they shot at me."

Jake sat down and held her close.

"Slow down, Daisy. A dead body?"

"It was awful. I don't know how to describe it. There were bugs, maggot." Daisy trailed off and leaned into Jake. "You were right. I was so stupid."

"No darlin', you were so brave. If you hadn't gone out there that body might never've been discovered. And you're safe now. Not looking too good, if I can say so."

Daisy sniffled. "You think so?"

"Naw darlin', you look just fine." He smiled. "Oh, you mean the 'brave' part? Yep, Meant every word. Just wish you'd invited me along."

Lucas and Ed came in. Lucas was using his cane again.

"Daisy, are you all right?" Lucas said as he sat on the couch as well and hugged her.

Daisy nodded.

"You'll stay with me for the time being. In your old

room. You can even bring that dang cat over. Jake can get it."

"Okay."

"We'll go over later to get your clothes. I don't want you going anywhere alone until the person who did all this is behind bars. Jake?"

"Going now."

Jake left and Ed gently helped Daisy up and to her room. It was upstairs across from his.

As they were leaving, Lucas asked, "Are you gonna be all right?"

"Yes, Daddy. Thank you."

"We'll let you rest up then."

Daisy looked around the room she had grown up in. When she returned from college, she chose the garage apartment as her own. This bedroom had too many memories of the time when her mother was still alive, and Daisy could not bear it. She removed her shoes, lay down on one of the twin beds, and fell asleep.

CHAPTER 41

The cat purred loudly enough in Daisy's ear to wake her. Daisy snatched her and held her high. For a second, she thought about hurling her to the floor, but instead looked into her eyes and said, "You're a persistent little thing, aren't you? How did you get here?"

The stray blinked.

"I'm persistent too. And besides, you did alert me when someone broke into my place."

Another blink.

"If you are going to stay with me, you'll need a name. I'll think on it."

She put the cat down and sat on the side of the bed. Seeing the litter box, she pointed and said, "However, we'll have to do something about that. I can't have kitty litter all over my bathroom."

Daisy put on her shoes and they both went down to the kitchen.

Retta was alone, sitting at the table. "Good morning, dear."

"Where is everyone?" Daisy sat at the table too. The cat jumped on top of it. Daisy just shook her head at it.

"It's Sunday, you remember, and your father and Ed went to early church. Said to tell you they'd be home around noon. Jasmine got here last night after you had gone to bed. You just missed her. And Walker is still asleep."

"Is Jasmine planning to stay here?"

"I think she's going to their house. She's inclined to move us back before she drives back to Atlanta. Doesn't think it's necessary for them to be here."

Daisy opened her mouth to argue but realized she would be preaching to the choir so instead she just said, "I want you to feel safe."

The cat stuck out one hind leg and began to clean itself.

"I know, dear, and I appreciate it. Anyhow let me get you some breakfast. Do you drink coffee?"

"Yes."

Retta went to the kitchen counter and the cat followed, weaving in and out of her legs.

"I guess you are hungry too."

The cat meowed in response so Retta first prepared her a bowl of milk and set it on the floor away from where she would be cooking. She put strips of bacon in a cast iron skillet, and while that was sizzling, she diced some potatoes and onions for hash browns. She turned the bacon over and pressed the potato and onion mixture to one side of the skillet. After she flipped the hash browns, she took out the bacon and set it on paper towels to remove some of the fat. She cracked two eggs to fry sunny side up.

Daisy was still sitting quietly at the table when Retta placed the plate and a mug of coffee in front of her.

"I think I'll call it Rescue. What do you think? I guess I'm rescuing her from something, and she rescued me, sort of, when she let me know someone had been in my apartment."

"That's very clever. So she's a female?"

"I don't know. She acts like one, poking her nose into everything and…."

"Why men do that too, dear! Let's see." Retta lifted Rescue to look at her genitals and pronounced that Rescue was indeed a girl.

"You'll be having kittens unless you have her spayed. In fact, it might already be too late for that."

With that she put Rescue on the floor and sat down with Daisy.

"Eat your breakfast."

As Daisy began to eat, she realized she was ravenous. She only had a snack on Saturday.

"They told me you found a body on the mountain," Retta began. "They said it was a man?"

"Yes." Daisy recoiled at the memory of the man, his

swollen and discolored face, the maggots and ants everywhere. She felt nauseous at the thought but recovered herself and said, "I'm sure he was the second man I saw, the one running away from the crash."

"You didn't recognize him?"

"I thought I did, for just a second, but the way he was dressed, he wasn't from Franklin."

Retta's body relaxed as she drew a deep breath.

"Why?" Daisy's training and instincts made her suspicious about Retta's question and apparent relief at Daisy's answer.

"Well, I haven't seen Judas for several days. I was worried."

"It wasn't him unless he got some new clothes."

Jude, like most of the locals in Franklin, wore blue jeans and flannel shirts that were usually well worn. Daisy spared Retta from the fact that the corpse was so badly decomposed as to be unidentifiable. She was saved from having to discuss it further when they heard a truck pull up outside. Jake soon entered the great room.

"Daisy! I did not expect to see you up with the morning birds," he said. "How are you?"

"I'm okay. I want to go to my place. Can you bring the litter box?"

"Darlin', your wish is my command."

Daisy picked up Rescue; Jake retrieved the litter box from the bedroom; and they left Retta alone with her thoughts.

"I was just at the hospital morgue. They took the

body there this morning, and from the dental work they don't think he was from Franklin, or even Macon County."

"How could they tell that, from teeth?"

"Sheriff said it was the way the crowns had been done. He had two on his molars, and they were gold-capped, flashy, not porcelain like we have here. They'll check with the dentists here tomorrow, but Sheriff said they are very sure about this."

"It was the other man from the plane. The one I saw running away."

Jake said, "You're probably right, so you don't have to keep looking for him, do you?"

"I know I'm right," Daisy replied, "but that leaves the question of who killed him and why? And who shot at me as I was running away?"

Jake took Daisy by the shoulders and made her look him in the eyes. "Those are matters for the sheriff and the FBI, Daisy. You could have been killed up there."

"I know, Jake. You are right. I won't get involved with that investigation, but I can't stay cooped up here all the time, can I? I've still got the feature story about de Soto to finish. Jake, Daddy told me why Mom was on that road the day she died."

"You're kidding. What did he tell you?"

"Do you remember when a cheerleader from Asheville disappeared. Dad told me that she thought the girl might have been kidnapped. Well, someone tipped her off that she might be held captive in the forest off that road, and she was going to try to find her on the day she disappeared."

"Daisy, please don't say you are going to look for it?"

"I have to."

"Well, darlin', just promise you won't go without me. And I think we both should take guns, just in case."

"I promise," Daisy pledged. "Can we go in the morning?"

"Sure thing, but before we go, I want to make sure you remember how to use a gun."

"Okay. I'll meet you at the farm after lunch. I've got to see Lexie about something first."

CHAPTER 42

Daisy dodged potholes as she drove down the once-graveled lane to Lexie and Ralph's farm on the Cartoogechaye Creek. They put their entire resources into the bookstore and their house. New gravel could come later.

Yellow, red, and orange leaves scattered through the tree branches to signal the end of the Indian summer they had been enjoying. By Thanksgiving, the trees would be bare save for the deep burnt orange and magentas of the red and white oaks. Many of those leaves would fade to brown and linger on branches until banished by spring's new growth.

Cylinders of hay baled in a third cut remained in the fields. The first cuttings were stored in an old barn on the farm, but these had been sold to another farmer who had yet to pick them up. Money made from the sale would go into improvements to the farm and the bookstore.

A new stable had already been built using funds from last year's hay. It stood to the side of the house they were renovating. It included a studio apartment for a stable boy, and that is where Lexie and Brad were living until renovations had been completed. They hoped they could move in time to hold a Thanksgiving feast for their friends.

Daisy walked around to the rear of the building and knocked on the sole door. Sunday was the only day the bookstore was closed so still in her nightgown and robe and holding a mug of coffee, Lexie opened the door.

"Daisy! I wasn't expecting to see you today."

"I have to talk to you. Can I come in?"

"Of course. Have you eaten yet? We were about to have dinner."

"No thanks, but don't let me stop you," Daisy said. "You didn't make it to church?"

"Nope, yesterday was too exhausting. Keira didn't come in, so I had to work at the coffee bar as well as in the bookstore. With the break in the weather, we had nonstop customers."

Daisy joined them at the old oak dining table loaded with the customary Franklin Sunday dinner: fried chicken, mashed potatoes with gravy, turnip greens, biscuits, and a chess pie holding pride of place in the center of the table.

"Please eat," Daisy said, and Ralph took her at her word and dug in. Lexie waited for Daisy to speak.

"Do you remember what I told you at the store? About Joe Taylor and the drugs? About the man I saw running away from the plane?"

"Of course, I'm not likely to forget any of that, am I?"

"I think I found the man yesterday. Dead!"

Ralph stopped eating at this. "Where was this?

Daisy answered, "In a cave near the road where Mom died, and that's not all. Someone else shot at me. I'm sure one of them must have been the other man I saw at the crash."

"Who do you think could have been the second man?"

"I wish I knew."

"Have you told the sheriff?"

Daisy nodded.

"He knows."

Daisy took a deep breath, leaned back, exhaled, and said, "You won't believe this either. Dad has finally told me what Mom was doing out there."

Lexie's eyes widened and Brad put his fork down.

"You're kidding," Lexie said.

"My mother received a report from Social Services in Asheville that a young girl had been reported as missing and had last been seen in Franklin. The girl was a cheerleader named Amy. Mom was working with Child Protective Services in Asheville and then also in Atlanta to try to find out what could have happened to her. They came up with a list of girls who were still unaccounted for.

"Then on the day she had the car accident, she received an anonymous tip that the girl was being held at an old cabin in the woods off that road. She called Dad to tell him that she was going to check it out. That was the last time he spoke with her.

"It came out later that she had learned the names of at least eight young girls still missing, and that was just for the four years that I was away in Chapel Hill."

"So, there could be more." Ralph stated.

"Yes. They leave if they don't see a future here.

"When Dad told me why my other had gone up there, I decided to take a look, to see if I could find signs of the cabin. That's where I was when someone took a shot at me. I was in the woods halfway between the Walker farm and the Simpsons' mine."

Lexie said, "You know I've got a lot of faith in you as a reporter, but I agree with Lucas and Jake. You need to let Ben and the FBI agent handle all these things, the crash, the murders, everything. You need to tell them everything you know. Everything! Then you need to drop it. Will you do that, Daisy?"

"I just can't promise that, Lexie. I feel like I am getting so close to finding out why my mother died. I don't believe it was an accident. She knew how to drive on any kind of road in the mountains. The weather was good. There is no way it was an accident. She was murdered and I believe either the Walkers or the Simpsons were involved, just as they are involved with the drug smuggling going on around here now."

Lexie shook her head. "You think I don't understand how you feel, but I do. You feel you've been lied to, that no one else wanted to discover what happened, but that's not true. It was thoroughly investigated at the time and the conclusion was that it was an accident. Lucas didn't give you details because he wanted to spare you from worrying. He had made clear his concerns at the time. Listen, Brad reviewed the case file and he found nothing in it pointing to anything other than an accident."

Daisy's chest heaved with a deep sigh.

"I can't promise to stop looking into it, but I promise I will try not to go out investigating in the woods by myself.

CHAPTER 43

The next tropical storm was hurtling through the Gulf states to the southwest and was rapidly pushing out the fresh air brought in by the cold front. By noon, an oppressive humidity, too warm for late October in the mountains, replaced the cool crisp air of yesterday's cold front.

Jake had been working to rehab the farmhouse and had planted a small vegetable garden, full of greens and root vegetables. When Daisy knocked on the door at the house, Clemmie Smith answered the door.

"Daisy dear, come in."

"Thank you, Mrs. Smith. Just for a minute. Is Jake around?"

"He's out back in the garden patch. He told me you

two are going to do some target practice. Please tell him I said to come back so you can have some lunch with us when you're finished."

Daisy thanked her and went to find Jake. Before she even reached the path to the garden, she heard Suzie Q barking to alert her master that an intruder was approaching. The dog bounded out of the thicket and immediately started wildly waving her rear back and forth in excitement at seeing Daisy. When she finally reached her, she flopped on her back with four legs in the air and pawed at Daisy.

"Okay, okay, Suzie, I guess you need a belly rub desperately, huh? Jake too busy to give you attention?"

When she had had enough love from Daisy, Suzie Q leaped up and baying excitedly signaled to Jake that she had found something great. The Redbone hound disappeared into the thicket she had come from, and Daisy followed.

Jake was given the dog by a neighbor who had sold the rest. Suzie was the runt of a ten-pup litter and almost did not survive. She struggled unsuccessfully for a teat until Clemmie Smith volunteered to take her in and bottle feed her. Jake soon took over the nighttime and early morning feedings. By the time to wean her from the bottle, she was following at Jake's heels whenever he was on the farm.

When Daisy reached them, the hound was lying on the ground at the end of the row where Jake was using a long-handled plow to deepen the furrows between rows of vegetables.

"I thought it might be you. Suzie Q doesn't raise such a ruckus for anybody else."

Daisy squatted beside the dog to scratch behind her ears. "I'm flattered! What are you doing?"

"I'm hoping the rains would destroy what's left of this crop."

He put away the plow, wiped off the sweat with a towel, and put on his shirt, leaving it open. His body was lean and taut.

"Take this," he said, handing Daisy a shotgun. He grabbed a pistol and a couple of boxes of ammunition. "Suzie Q, go home."

The hound walked slowly to the path toward the farmhouse and disappeared. Daisy and Jake walked together through the garden clearing to a path through the woods.

"I've fired a gun before, you know."

No reply

"I come from a long line of hunters. The first McLarens had to hunt to survive, no Walmart or Ingles back then. They hunted daily unless they got a deer. Then they'd feast for days, drying and smoking what they couldn't eat, stretching and tanning the hide, using the antlers to make tools and weapons. The Cherokee had taught them that.

"All the first settlers had to hunt to survive in the new wilderness.

"When I was old enough, Mama and Daddy got me a rifle and took me out with them to hunt deer. They only killed one. Daddy said it was to get venison and to cull the deer population. We packed our freezer full of venison to use until the next winter."

"Let's get to work," Jake interrupted her reminiscences. He had left the family farm as soon as he was old enough, and, when he inherited it, did not move back until after his father had left. Daisy knew that his memories of his childhood were nightmares of abuse and neglect, with no protection from his mother who was suffering as well. The two of them had come a long way since then.

"Turn here."

They walked through the path in the woods to another small clearing where Jake had set up cans and bottles on a fallen log.

"It's a lot different to shoot a deer than to shoot at a man, even if you are just trying to scare him off. Here, put these in and load the shotgun."

Jake gave her earplugs and the gun, and she put a cartridge in each chamber.

"Now aim at the cans on the far right of the log and pull the trigger when you have it sighted."

Daisy put the gun to her shoulder and lined up the sight with the cans.

"Whoa, darlin', not like that unless you want to tear your shoulder." Jake stopped her. "Move it over to your chest, just below your collarbone."

Daisy repositioned the weapon.

"Now, hold it tight against your chest, lean forward, sight up the cans again," he instructed. "That looks good. Now pull the trigger once."

The single blast took off half the rotten log with the cans.

"Now if they keep coming at you, you've got another shot before you have to reload. Get ready again."

Daisy duplicated her previous actions.

"Perfect, now pull!"

The second shot took off more cans, some bottles, and a sizeable chunk of the log.

Daisy was excited about her success. "Not bad, am I?" she fished for a compliment.

"Actually, I'm proud of you. Now I want you to find some cover to get behind and practice shooting from there."

"You mean we aren't finished?"

"You did really well, but our goal here is for you to have a way to protect yourself—if you have to. You don't want to go looking for trouble, I hope, and you sure don't want to make yourself an easy target. Take these. I'll be back in about thirty minutes to see how you are doing."

Jake gave her the box of cartridges.

"Where are you going?"

"To the garden. I've got a lot of work to do before the storm."

Daisy took the box and watched Jake disappear into the path. She kneeled behind a bush on the left side of the clearing and reloaded the barrels. She experimented with positions and soon realized that to get into the correct posture to shoot, she would have to get out from behind the bush prepared to fire.

After more experimentation she discovered the most efficient way to do this was to sit with her back to the bush and lean her head out to see what was happening behind her. When she decided to fire, she would close the action, swing out, stand, and pull the trigger.

She was still practicing when Jake tapped her on her shoulder. She removed the ear plugs.

"Looks like you've torn up that log, darlin'. Not bad. Let's take a break and then you can try the pistol. Mom has some lunch ready for us."

Jake's mother had set out lunch on the screen porch, chicken salad and grilled cheese sandwiches with bowls of homemade tomato soup.

"I made the soup from the last of the summer tomatoes and froze it," she told them. "Now eat up. You need to finish that garden work this afternoon. I think the storm might get here earlier than they're saying."

Back in the clearing Jake handed Daisy the handgun.

"It's a Sig Sauer P228, my father got it when he was in the Army. I have a feeling it just disappeared and ended up in his trunk when his tour ended."

"Is it loaded?"

"Not yet," Jake said. "Practice a little before we put ammo in it. Take hold of it like this."

He grasped the handle with three fingers and laid his index finger along the barrel.

"Like this?"

"Now with your other hand, pull the slide back. That will release a bullet into the chamber when you have a magazine loaded."

Jake continued to work with Daisy until she was comfortable with the weapon. Then he loaded a mag and handed her the Sig Sauer. "Remember what I told you and try not to rush. Take a deep breath and begin. Relax your shoulders. Line up the target with the front sight."

Daisy proceeded perhaps a bit too cautiously and was still unprepared for the upward kick of the handgun. Anticipating a push back against her as she had experienced with the shotgun, she tensed at the last moment and missed the target.

"I'll never be able to use this."

"I've never known you to give up so easily, darlin'. Let's keep going."

Daisy groaned but fired again and again until Jake was satisfied.

CHAPTER 44

Daisy took Wayah Road toward Franklin, but instead of turning right at Loafer's Glory she turned left to take the Old Murphy Road into town. Even though she had not gone this way in ages, she recognized landmarks which remained. Cartoogechaye Elementary School, the dollar store, and the recovery center. Several rusted-out mobile homes resisted demolition and stood defiantly as various mountain vines twined around them.

Passing by the Appalachian Animal Rescue Center Thrift Shop, Daisy thought that the rescue center would take the little stray cat in. She had written a story for the *Free Press* reporting that it was a no-kill shelter which relied on public support to maintain operations. Adoption fees covered the costs of neutering, spaying, and vaccinations. Surely, they could find a good home for the calico.

As she passed Noah's Ark, she had the idea that she could help by having her spayed and vaccinated before taking her to the shelter. That would save time and money that could go to the care of other unwanted animals. Definitely the best idea.

When she reached the town city limits, the name of the road changed to Palmer Street. She took the first turn where she could cut across to Harrison Avenue and the part of town where she lived.

All the way home she thought about Keira. Lexie hired her because she had the reputation of being reliable, a student who consistently made A grades. It was not like her to blow off work and especially, to do it without notifying Lexie or Brad. What if she had obtained some of the heroin that killed Joe Taylor? She was not the type to use drugs, but then neither was Joe. Perhaps she should tell Nathan Stark her concerns.

As she pulled into the driveway, she thought about dropping by Lucas's. Ed was certain to have catfish and hush puppies, their usual Friday night supper. Corn bread and turnip greens on the side. Tempting as the idea was, she went straight to her garage apartment. She rationalized that she had to feed Rescue, but truth was she was exhausted from the stress of the week.

Dumping everything but her cell on the couch, she called Nathan Stark. No answer. She did not leave a voicemail. Keira had probably been out late Friday night and slept late. Teenagers were known to sleep until the afternoon so why should Keira be an exception. She would probably show up with a hang-dog look on Monday, and she would certainly resent having the law show up on her doorstep thus bringing her parents into the situation.

Daisy left her phone on the bed and went to get something to make a sandwich. As she shut the refrigerator door, she realized that Rescue was not doing her usual act of twirling between her legs.

"Rescue? Here kitty, kitty."

Her feline companion had probably discovered a new hiding place and was lurking there waiting to pounce as Daisy passed. Daisy heated a skillet as she slathered mayonnaise on bread slices, put a cheese slice on one, closed the sandwich and buttered each side. The sandwich sizzled as it hit the skillet. She smashed it as one side browned, then flipped it and smashed the other side. This was her favorite way of making grilled cheese. She thought hers was better even than Stamey's.

She watched the Weather Channel as she ate her sandwich. Another tropical storm was forecast for the following day, but it would not reach Franklin until late afternoon or evening. Her cell chimed.

"Hello, Daisy. This is Nathan. You called me?"

Darn.

"Yes, but it's nothing."

"It must be something or you wouldn't be calling me on Sunday night."

He was right. She had been worried enough about

Keira to call in the first place so she should tell him now.

"I saw Lexie and Brad today, you know, they own the bookstore. They told me how hard work was yesterday because Keira Swan didn't come to work her shift at the coffee bar."

"And?"

"That's just not like Keira. It's so out of character. That's why I thought about telling you. Then I remembered the foolish things teenagers can do and thought it best to wait and see."

"Thanks for letting me know. I'll look into it."

She finished her sandwich and carried the plate to the kitchen counter.

Still no Rescue and she was beginning to worry. She called out for her and telephoned Lucas to see if Rescue were there. Flashlight in hand she searched the driveway and bushes to the rear of the garage. No luck.

There could not be many places to hide in this small apartment. Under the bed? She got on her knees and peered into the dark space. No Rescue. Daisy was about to give up when she noticed the closed closet door. Surely not.

When she opened the door, Rescue ran out. "Yowl." She dashed to her litter box, now placed in a corner of the bedroom.

"Mystery solved. But what were you doing in there?'

Apparently, the calico had been busy while hidden away. She had pulled several cotton sweaters from shelves and created a soft bed in a corner in the back of the closet. Daisy picked up the sweaters, folded them, and placed them back on a shelf.

"Crazy cat! I guess you'll want some supper now."

Rescue narrowed her eyes as she looked over her shoulder at Daisy. She did her business and scratched to cover it up, once again strewing litter around the box.

Daisy returned to the kitchen with Rescue following close behind.

She filled one bowl with fresh water which the cat slurped up greedily. Then she opened a Fancy Feast for another bowl. The cat circled between her ankles before settling down to eat.

Daisy returned to bed. It was quite a while before she could get to sleep. She lay there thinking about Keira and hoping her worries were needless. Surely, Keira was well and would turn up for work on Monday. Daisy would go by the bookstore to check on her and tease her about her lapse in reliability.

CHAPTER 45

No alarm roused Daisy from a deep sleep. She had exhausted herself on the previous day with busy-ness which accomplished nothing, like Sisyphus pushing a granite boulder uphill for hours only to have it come crashing back down on him, each time pushing him closer and closer to the bottom of a cliff face that resembled the sharpest drop to the fast-rushing waters that had carved out the Cullasaja Gorge.

In the dream she was a Cherokee princess being dragged through brambles and laurel ivy by de Soto. Again and again, she tried to stand and run behind him but kept pitching forward into fallen oaks split and rotting in the rain. The blackberry thorns snatched her clothes and carved blood-red claw marks on her cheeks.

Suddenly, a firm hand hoisted her onto a sleek black stallion and galloped away from de Soto and his men. As they raced along, the rain came down in sharp pellets blown by the storm stabbing her face that was already scratched and bloodied by the brambles. They were riding along the narrow edge of the gorge when her savior turned and grinned. She did not know him. Peering over the precipice to the rain-swollen river rushing a thousand feet below, she had no choice but to fasten her arms around his waist and wait for what was to come.

Rescue was not in her usual spot under the covers when Daisy awoke. In the span of a week, she had become a comforting presence in the apartment, padding around behind Daisy and entwining herself around Daisy's legs. The cat's rhythms were Daisy's rhythms. She slept when Daisy slept. She nestled in front of her food to eat when Daisy sat with her meals at the small round table or on the couch to eat while watching TV. When Daisy wrote on her laptop at night in bed, or scrolled through Tweets and Googled various topics, Rescue would snooze beside her and purr loudly in feline satisfaction. When the lights were finally turned off, and Daisy finally fell asleep, the cat would push gently under the covers and snuggle in the crook formed by Daisy's folded knees.

Daisy felt for Rescue but soon remembered that the cat had been in the closet when Daisy returned from her work. Cold she be there again? Groaning and rolling over, she longed to drag the covers up and over her head to shut out the morning and sleep in, then she remembered the impending tropical storm and propelled herself out of bed.

As she walked toward the bathroom Rescue appeared, emerging from the closet bending and stretching her limbs like a yogi saluting the sun. She had once again made a nest of sweaters.

"As soon as this storm passes through, you're off to the vet."

In the shower she thought about the previous day's events. Jake was growing even more protective of her than usual. She was not sure how she felt about that. She felt very contented spending time with Jake and his mother at their farm, but she regretted her promise to Lexie to not keep investigating by herself.

The logical thing to do today would be to call Jake and get him to accompany her, but she bristled at the thought. Jake could be brought in if she sensed danger. She had already forgotten about the terror she felt when someone shot at her. She had not even been wounded let alone come close to dying. She rationalized that Jake had to work and that she had to get a lot completed before the storm began.

Daisy thought about Nathan Stark who took her concerns seriously and seemed to respect her as a professional reporter with a job to do. She was glad he had contacted him about Keira. She thought about her mother's enquiries into the disappearance of other girls. Daisy had been so distraught about her mother's death that it never occurred to her to take up the investigation, to learn whether or not more girls had disappeared without any warning to their families or friends. Now she was very worried. What she knew about Keira did not suggest any reason for Keira to run away.

Out of the shower she texted Lexie, "Let me know when you hear from Keira. Are you closing the shop before the storm gets here?"

She dressed and prepared breakfast for herself and Rescue, who was looking healthier and plumper. A ding announced the reply from Lexie, "K and yes." There remained nothing else she could do for Keira until she heard from Lexie if she came to work.

Upon leaving the apartment, she was careful to leave the calico inside. The cat had been behaving so weirdly so she was relieved that she had appeared to eat breakfast. Although Daisy planned to be home when the heavens opened to unleash stormy weather on the valley, she feared it would begin before she could make it back, and she hated the idea that Rescue might be lost in the storm. She had not needed to concern herself because, having finished her own breakfast, Rescue was once more not in her sight. She locked the door and walked down the steps to her car.

The driveway was empty. Lucas had already left for his office, so Daisy would call him from the road. She was impatient to begin her search for clues, for answers to the questions the past week had created for her. She could not get Keira out of her mind and decided to contact Social Services if she did not show up at the bookstore that morning.

Storms had moved into the county during the night.

Dark low-lying clouds covered the mountain ridges while a thick fog formed a layer on the Little Tennessee River. In between these layers there was sunshine and a clear view of the valley and lower mountains. As the day progressed the predicted heavy rains would enshroud the entire area and conceal both animal and man who dared to move about.

CHAPTER 46

The days without rain had let the crops, mainly alfalfa and corn, dry out. A new threat to the harvest, fueled by a late-season tropical storm, was making its way into the valley, and the farmers were taking advantage of the time before the heavy rains would begin to harvest the late corn and to make round bales of hay to leave in the fields for the coming winter.

Daisy had always enjoyed observing the mowing and baling of hay. During her summer vacations she had visited her aunt and uncle who kept a small herd of Black Angus. She did her part by helping her aunt tend to the daily farm chores. Daisy had a hard time deciding which was her favorite thing to do. She began each day at the hen house, strewing cracked corn for their breakfast and gathering eggs for her aunt. The fresh eggs would be used up by the end of the day for breakfast omelets, bread and cake baking, cookies for Daisy; those left would be added to the mash for piglets who were being weaned.

Next, she would fetch the slop bucket by the kitchen door. The leftover vegetables would be a treat for the few pigs they kept for breeding. During harvesting they were kept in stalls in the stable along with the horses, Rainbow and Sunshine. Daisy would provide all with bales of hay, then treat the hog and sow with portions of the slop. The horses would get alfalfa cubes to munch on.

Daisy approached the first of several fields she would pass on the way home. The sunshine-filled week had allowed the fields to dry, and they had been mowed and raked.

In the first and second cuts of the year the hay was packed into smaller square bales to be stored and sold locally. The farmers were glad to get this third cut which they would leave in the fields to later unroll for the cattle. This was a good harvest, and the farmers should be able to go all winter without having to buy additional hay.

She turned her thoughts back to Louisa and tried to figure out what to do with what she saw. She knew she could not just forget about Louisa, and now to add to her worries young Keira Swan had disappeared. Her mother had died while trying to find young women who had vanished without a trace. Keira's failure to work her shift at the bookstore coffee bar brought thoughts of her mother top of mind once more. Ruminations about her mother's death filled and confused her thoughts.

Jake would tell her to let it be, to let the sheriff and the FBI handle it. One minute she did not think it warranted a visit from Ben or Nathan; the next minute she thought it did. She had confided in Nathan Stark her concerns about Keira, and he had pledged to investigate. The FBI had resources she lacked. They would be able to fly over the woods that would soon be stripped of its autumn leaves. They would be able to see any remote and seemingly unreachable cabins.

She almost missed her turn but at the last minute darted into the exit lane to make a sharp turn onto the exit ramp closest to downtown and headed towards Lucas's law office. He would know what to do. She got Siri to call him.

"Dad, I need your advice about something. Can I come to your office?"

"I'm just about to go into Rollie Pollies for breakfast. Want to join me?"

"I'll be there in a minute."

Downtown Franklin was quiet. Daisy pulled into a diagonal parking space in front of the café. She thought about calling Lexie, but the bookstore would not open until ten, and Keira would not be there until it had opened. Lexie had promised to let Daisy know once she heard from Keira. Daisy did not want to become a nuisance to her friend.

She still hoped her worried were unwarranted, that

Keira would go to work at the bookstore with profuse apologies for not calling to let Lexie and Brad know where she had been. That Louisa and her sons had nothing to do with the plane crash, drugs. That they know nothing about the person who had fired on her.

Daisy waved to Lucas and got out of the car. She was careful to lock it, a precaution she would never have thought about taking a week ago, especially on Main Street. During the years she remained in Macon County, she had grown to feel secure, safe, confident that she dwelled among people who knew her and who wished her well, among friends. In the course of one week that assumption had disintegrated, to be replaced by fear and doubt, a pervasive belief that she was surrounded by danger, by threats to her life and possibly to the lives of those around her, to her friends, and possibly even to Lucas. A miasma of confusion and hostility threatened to enclose her as the heavy gray clouds drew closer and closer to Franklin.

As she regarded the few people out early on Main Street, she wondered if they were really tourists come to look for gems to take back home and show off the treasures to be had in the mountains of North Carolina, or were they shadowing her. Did they mean her harm? Could they be the very people bringing drugs into the county? Could they have harmed Joe and maybe Keira?

Daisy pushed all thoughts out of her mind, save for those about Keira Swan and Louisa Simpson. She approached her father with a smile. Lucas was her true north, the constant she could rely on to protect her, to keep her safe, even when she resisted his advice. She might disagree with him, but she rarely argued. She would do anything for him, just as he would do the same for her.

The father and daughter hugged each other, then Lucas opened the door for Daisy to enter the small restaurant ahead of him.

CHAPTER 47

Rockin' Rollie Pollies was quiet. A few gem-seeking retirees, undaunted by the prediction of a tropical storm, sat quietly enjoying a hearty breakfast before driving to one of the many gem mines for a day of treasure seeking. Locals would begin to drift in as it got closer to noon.

Daisy and Lucas took one of the booths along the wall, and immediately a waitress approached them with menus and glasses of water.

"Good morning, Beth," Lucas said.

"Back at you, Lucas. Hey Daisy."

"We know what we want, Beth," Daisy said. "I'll have a cheese omelet with whole what toast, and…."

Lucas peered over his glasses at Beth and then at

Daisy. "I reckon I'll take the omelet too." He glanced at Daisy again. "And I suppose I'll have whole wheat toast as well."

"Sure thing, and what to drink?"

Daisy answered, "We'll both have coffee—and we'll share some hash browns."

Ordinarily, she would have guilted Lucas into no hash browns or coffee. His doctor had warned him to watch his weight and his diet, or risk a heart attack, but today she eased up because she was going to need his assistance and wanted him to be in a good mood. They chatted while waiting for their order.

"Thank you for meeting me, Daddy. It looks like the weather's going to turn earlier than they thought."

"I told Maxie not to bother coming in today and I'm going to get some files to work on at home and then close the office around noon. I think Ed will stay over tonight. What time will you be done for the day?"

"I'm planning to get home before the storm starts. I don't want to get caught on a mountain like I was during the last one."

Beth put their plates before them. "Y'all need anything else?"

"No thanks."

They ate in silence until Lucas asked, "What's wrong, Daisy? You know I can still tell when you're going do something you know I won't approve of? Your mother had the same look. Usually meant she was going to spoil you with more clothes you didn't need."

Daisy hung her head. She had suddenly begun to

feel like that same girl who needed and wanted her mother, desperately now. Teardrops welled in her eyes, but she brushed them off. Now was not the time to think about her mother.

"I'm very worried about Louisa. She looks horrible. Her hair's a mess. She looks like she's fixing to cry at any second. She isn't being her usual smart-alecky self.

"And worse than that, she looks scared. Louisa's never afraid."

"Why do you think that is?" Lucas said.

"I'm sure it has something to do with whatever has been going on with the Walkers and the plane crash. And I know it has to do with drugs. Nathan doesn't say they are involved, but I'm sure they are."

Lucas took her hand and said gently, "Now look, I know you think it falls on you to fix everything, to solve every mystery in Franklin, but it's not. Leave this to professionals who know what they are doing. Call Nathan. Tell him what you've just seen and let him handle it."

"I know you're right. I actually called him last night, and he gave me the same advice."

The floodgates opened and Daisy began to sob. Lucas moved to the bench beside her and held her close.

"There, there," he said, "everything will be okay. You have got to let this go. You've been through too much this week."

Daisy sobbed against his shoulder and then composed herself.

Their order arrived and did not disappoint. As they ate, Daisy continued.

"That's not the only thing. You know how Mom was trying to find out why girls from Franklin were disappearing?"

"Of course."

"Keira Swan has been missing since Saturday. I'm so afraid she has been taken, or maybe used some of the same heroin that killed Joe Taylor. Lexie is supposed to let me know if she comes for her shift today."

"What happened to Joe was a terrible thing, but do you have any evidence that would connect Keira and Joe?"

"Not hard evidence, but they could have become close at the bookstore. They could've been seeing each other. Keira might be depressed since Joe died and …."

"You're right. These could be reasons to worry about Keira, but you even admit they are not evidence. They are hunches. You know the difference.

"Daisy, I'm worried more about you. You are obsessing over Keira, and you need to let it go. At least until you hear if she goes to work at the bookstore today. Deal?"

"I'll try," she said grudgingly, knowing how difficult it would be to forget about young Keira.

"I'm sure she'll turn up. In the meantime, why don't you focus on your regular reporting and let Ben and Nathan Stark handle any more investigations into both of these matters. Okay?"

"Okay. I'll call Nathan as soon as I get to the office," she said while thinking, "Right after I get Louisa to a safe place."

Daisy left Lucas to finish his morning paper. Outside the sky was dark, and a drizzle had left a misty veil on her windshield. She set the windshield wipers to a slow intermittent timing.

To get to the Simpson Ruby Mine before the storm broke, she would have to hurry. From the Appalachian Parkway she could see isolated areas where sheets of rain were falling, but she estimated she had a couple of hours to complete her work for the day before returning to the safety of Lucas's property.

Retta Walker was not in danger since she was at Lucas's, and Daisy would soon hear from Lexie if Keira had reappeared on the scene. She would convince Louisa Simpson to join Retta, then she would question her one more time about the plane crash and that would conclude her research.

Then she would be able to keep her promise to her father.

CHAPTER 48

The parking lot at the ruby mine was empty except for the family trucks. A heavy chain still blocked the entrance, and Daisy parked the Jeep parallel to it. A light rain had begun to fall so she covered her head with her bag and rushed inside the store.

She was shocked to see how much Louisa's appearance had changed in the week since the plane had crashed a few miles above her mine. Her face held deep furrows between her eyebrows. Her hair was oily and messy as if a brush had not touched it in days. In fact, her whole appearance was disorganized and unkempt. Far from looking arrogant and annoyed to see Daisy, Louisa looked worried, almost frightened, and Daisy wondered why. She noticed that Louisa glanced nervously at the staircase leading to the apartment upstairs.

"Morning, Louisa," Daisy said.

"Morning, Daisy," Louisa whispered back. "Have you decided to try your luck today?"

Daisy smiled at that. Louisa was still selling in spite of all that had happened.

"No, ma'am, I just came to make sure you're okay," she said. "It's been such a crazy week. I still have a few questions about the plane crash, if you're up to talking about it."

Louisa said nothing. She just opened the cash register as if to take Daisy's money and give her a ticket. Daisy was unsure of how to tell Louisa that she was worried about Louisa's safety. She simply said, "How are you? I can't help but worry about you, after everything that's happened."

At that Louisa burst into tears and put her hand over her mouth to muffle her sobs.

Daisy was not prepared for this outburst. Fearing that she had intruded where she simply did not belong, she drew back, but as Louisa continued to wail, she hurried around the counter and put her arms around her.

"There, there," she said, "tell me about it."

Louisa's whole body shook with her sobs and Daisy held her even tighter. At last, Louisa stopped her crying and straightened herself. She pushed Daisy away. "It's none of your business. You best get going," she said, "if you ain't buying a ticket."

She shut the drawer and turned as though to check her supplies and used the opportunity to wipe away some of her tears.

"Louisa!"

"I said go. Buy a ticket or leave. I got things to do."

Daisy stayed put.

"Suit yourself," Louisa said and went about her business. "I got work to do."

The ruby mine was not yet open for business, but Louisa was already busy preparing for the day. Apparently, her sons would not get up early to help her set up, so Louisa had them fill buckets and set them by the sluice the night before.

Daisy followed her to the back room where a stack of filtering screens from the previous day lay waiting to be cleaned. She cleaned the screens with a wire brush to dislodge fine particles.

She startled Daisy when she said, "You know I once found a small ruby wedged into the corner of a screen tray, so I'm always extra careful around the edges."

Satisfied that the trays held no hidden treasures, she carried them to the front office and stacked them on the shelves behind her counter. It seemed to Daisy that Louisa was prattling on to avoid discussing the plane crash, the murders on the mountainside, or anything else of consequence.

Louisa returned to the back room where Daisy had remained. She opened the safe and retrieved the money tray, which she had prepared the night before, and a fresh roll of tickets. The color of the ticket rolls changed each day; this day was red. They were also numbered so her boys could make sure nobody was bringing in their own. Like most swindlers, Louisa believed everyone else was out to gyp her and acted accordingly.

The safe also contained the few large uncut gems her men had once found, rubies, emeralds, rose quartz. "This emerald would fetch a pretty price, but I hang on to it for a rainy day," she said as she closed the safe and returned to the front room. This time Daisy followed.

Setting the money tray and roll of red tickets on the counter, Louisa unlocked the cash register. After counting the money, she put a sheet of paper with the total and breakdown of dollars and coins on the bottom of the drawer. She set the tray on top of it.

She tore off a strip of tickets, put those in the drawer, and put the remaining roll under the counter. Finally, she closed and locked the drawer.

Louisa went to the sink in the back room. As she washed her hands, she looked at herself in the medicine cabinet mirror above the sink and saw the reflection of a sad old woman. It seemed to Daisy that overnight her eyes had sunk in and deep worry lines crisscrossed her brow. Louisa no longer made any attempt to fix her hair.

Daisy was convinced that Louisa had not been involved in whatever her husband and sons had brought into their business. Daisy could see that Louisa felt trapped by her circumstances. Her past and present hold misery, and she believes her future holds nothing.

Just then Jude, her middle son, came into the shop. He ignored Daisy and walked directly to the coffee maker.

"No coffee?"

"Hadn't had time. I can make some now if you'll put the sign out."

Jude gave his mother a disgusted look, but walked to the door, picked up the A-frame billboard, and went outside.

"And take down the chain."

Louisa made a pot of coffee and busied herself at the counter. She looked up but did not speak to Jude when he returned. Jude grabbed a mug of coffee and went upstairs without speaking.

Not knowing what to do and increasingly frustrated, Daisy said goodbye and left the store. Outside the winds whipped wildly about and the sky was already black with a low ceiling of clouds. This new storm had not provided the advance warning the last one had given. As predicted, it had arrived earlier than expected and would blow through Franklin. Perhaps it would throw a wrench in whatever schemes Jude might be planning.

Daisy's mind was racing. All the facts were coalescing—the plane crash, the influx of drugs into the small community, the murders—and the facts kept leading back to the two families dwelling on Ruby Mine Road. The Simpsons and the Walkers.

CHAPTER 49

The first heavy rains began as Daisy reached her home. Leaving the engine running, she raced into Lucas's house and went to the gun cabinet to retrieve her shotgun. As she punched in the code, she was surprised when Rescue began to rub between her ankles. Daisy could not resist picking her up for a quick cuddle.

"Who brought you over here? I guess they didn't want you to be stuck by yourself when the storm begins. I wish there were another way, Rescue, but I'm really afraid for Louisa," she said. The cat purripped back. "I'll bring her back soon, and you'll have one more person to adore you."

She set the calico cat on the floor. Taking a box of

buckshot shells from the gun locker, she closed it. Retta had come into the room while Daisy was preoccupied, and Daisy realized she should be worried about her as well. Walker and Simpson had made plans in Retta's kitchen, and they might decide they needed to cover their tracks completely.

"Retta, I'll explain in the car, but you need to come with me right now."

Daisy was shouting so frantically as she rushed to the door that Retta obeyed without questioning. In the Jeep Daisy told her to buckle her seat belt, and she did that, too, as Daisy circled around and left the driveway.

Daisy took the old Murphy highway to leave town. She tried to follow the speed limit until she could cross-over to the highway. She thought about what she should tell Retta about the recent occurrences in Franklin and decided to keep it simple. The simpler, the better.

The rains had begun but were not yet so heavy to make driving difficult. Daisy thought that the farmers had timed their baling just right. She took comfort in the fact that life in her high valley went on, beast and man performed their roles season after season--but she had no time for these reveries now. She had to reach Louisa and take her to safety.

Daisy glanced at Retta and saw her, with her dark eyes wide-eyed, hands braced on the door handle and seat. "I didn't mean to frighten you. Something is happening today. I'm worried about Louisa and want to pick her up and take you both back to Dad's house. Her son Jude was there, and I could tell something was wrong. Louisa was crying. I brought you in case I need help convincing her to come."

They both relaxed and, now on the Appalachian Parkway, Daisy floored the gas pedal. Few drivers were out now, all the locals having retreated to the security of their homes to ride out the tropical storm.

"I'm afraid he's got my husband into a scheme too big for him," Retta said out of the blue.

Daisy had no idea what she meant.

"Who? Simpson? What do you mean? Who are you talking about?"

"Not him. This man came from Atlanta; I think his name is Christopher or Christian. He spoke with an accent. Walker changed once he came on the scene."

Daisy took this in and asked, "Did he kill Caleb? This man, I mean, not Walker."

"I don't know. If he was around when that happened, he didn't come to the house. I don't think Walker knew him then. I just don't know."

Daisy removed one hand from the steering wheel and held Retta's hand for a moment.

"I promise I will find out who killed Caleb. I'll make sure the sheriff and the FBI agent don't forget about him."

Daisy slowed when she turned onto the road to the Simpsons' place.

"Can you tell me how your husband changed? What was he doing?"

Retta looked out the window at the rain that now blew almost parallel to the ground and at the trees in the fields that whipped wildly around.

"Its hard to say exactly how he was different. He had always been very secretive, but after that day he seldom spoke to me, and then he spoke just to tell me to stay in the house. He would tell me there was a bear with cubs in the area or make up some other excuse."

"How long this did go on?"

"For months. It ended when Caleb got shot."

"You saw that?"

Retta nodded.

"I rushed out to him. I couldn't believe it."

"Did you see who shot him?"

Retta shook her head.

"I just fell apart. I guess Walker got some tranquilizers for me. He moved Caleb's body. You know the rest."

Daisy shook her head in disbelief. Retta had to possess a strong core, a remarkable character to have come through this experience as well as she had.

"Do you know if anyone else was involved? How did this Christian find Walker?"

"I don't know. If I ever knew, I have forgotten. All I know is that once he came into our home, nothing was the same."

As Daisy searched for words to comfort Retta, she realized that she was starting to breathe rapidly, to hyperventilate, and she knew that she could not afford to let her anxiety control her. Louisa seemed to need her help, but maybe Louisa was part of these crimes. She could have taken advantage of Daisy's presence to leave the shop, but she did not.

Daisy summoned all her courage to shake off this doubt and the attending panic which the thoughts brought to concentrate on driving through the rain that from time to time would become heavy and blind her view of the road and traffic ahead. Daisy set the windshield wipers to the highest speed and continued to try to return to Louisa.

Beside her Retta Walker had relaxed a bit and peered ahead for obstacles on the highway.

As if she read Daisy's mind, she said, "I've known Louisa Simpson for most of her life. I have no doubt that Louisa has not taken part in anything her husband or sons have done. I've seen her with bruises often enough to know that her husband has abused her physically and verbally to the point that she couldn't resist them, much less stop their actions."

CHAPTER 50

Darkening clouds raced across the North Carolina sky as Daisy sped across the valley. The rain ceased from time to time, but the wind continued to blow stronger and stronger. The tropical storm had arrived as promised. Franklin was on the east side of the storm but, when windspeed was plus sixty miles per hour with gusts up to eighty-five or ninety, it mattered not. Tops of tulip poplar, pine, and young oaks careened wildly, sometimes circling in a counterclockwise direction. Majestic oaks that stood strong and proud for years swayed like metronomes to keep time with the wind.

The blasts of wind never came to a full stop but paused briefly before resuming with even stronger gusts. Then the tempest came on in full force, and as she drove on, the rains pounded against her car and the winds pushed her sideways. The storm continued thus, easing up and then attacking with a vengeance as the squall line advanced.

At last, she turned on the flashing hazard lights. She moved cautiously and stopped under an overpass to rest. The storm might cause the delivery of a new supply of heroin and other drugs to be delayed, or the scheduled flight could have been moved up and could already be at the small airport. Regardless Daisy could not be distracted from her current mission—to reach Louisa and get her to a safe place.

Daisy turned her red Jeep onto Ruby Mine Road. The open sign had been taken in and the parking lot was empty except for one truck. She parked, loaded her shotgun, and told Retta to stay in the car.

Daisy approached the store cautiously. She peered through one of the large display windows and saw no one. She tapped on the front door but got no reply. Everything seemed too still.

As she opened the door slightly, she called out, "Louisa?"

"Over here," came a faint hoarse response.

Daisy rushed over to the counter, shotgun at the ready, and looked over to see Louisa cradling her youngest, Joe, dead. Both were covered in blood. Louisa, ashen, white as the milky quartz from Franklin mines.

"Is anyone else here?" Daisy whispered, still clutching her weapon.

Louisa shook her head and looked up at Daisy with a question in her eyes, as if to ask if Daisy could make this all go away, turn time back to when they ran the mining business. When Louisa could be surly with customers and laugh with her boys at the supper table.

Daisy set her gun on the counter and walked around to Louisa. She gently pulled Joe's body from her and stretched him out as best she could. Then she crossed over to Louisa and helped her up. It was easy to do since Louisa had lost her spirit and offered no resistance.

Daisy had learned about *pathos* in her philosophy classes at college, but never before had she seen such a true example in real life. She gently escorted Louisa out to her Jeep. Putting a finger to her lips, she signaled Retta not to ask questions. Retta quietly helped Louisa into the back seat and climbed in on the other side to sit beside her.

Returning to the shop Daisy made sure no one else was there. She went upstairs to their living quarters and was not surprised it was as squalid as she had imagined, a kitchen with stove, sink and small refrigerator. Square table with four chairs. No couch or easy chair. Two bedrooms. Bath with clawfoot tub, toilet with seat up, and sink half-hanging off the wall. She did not take the time to look in the small, mirrored medicine cabinet before returning to her car.

Calmly and quietly, she asked, "Where have they gone? Is Jude with them?"

Shivering Louisa said, "I don't know."

Daisy thought that Walker must have killed Joe. She could not imagine a father or brother doing that although with these men anything might be possible.

"Where have they gone?'

No reply.

"Louisa, where are they going?"

"The airport." Louisa began to sob again.

"Are they leaving town?"

Again, no answer.

"Are they getting more drugs?" Daisy asked. She raised her voice and said, "Louisa!"

Louisa nodded.

"Heroin," she answered.

Daisy's worst fears were becoming reality. Heroin had already taken young Joe Taylor's life, and now a new supply was being imported. For all she knew, Keira Swan had taken the same drug and was lying dead somewhere, her body waiting to be discovered. Daisy suspected that Franklin was meant to be a midpoint stop for drugs intended for distribution in larger towns like Cullowhee, where Western Carolina University was located, Sylva, and Asheville. But someone held back enough to sell to adventurous teens, as well as the addicts who lived in town. She felt compelled to block this supply.

"We have to go to the airport," Daisy said. "We can't let more drugs come to Franklin, no matter who is involved in bringing it here. Are your seat belts fastened?"

Retta fastened her own and then reached over to secure Louisa's seatbelt. She took hold of Louisa's hand and held it tightly. Satisfied that they would be protected, Daisy left the Ruby Mine parking lot and accelerated to drive as fast as she could down the mountain road. She slowed to a safe speed on the hairpin curves and spots where the Jeep came too close to road edges with non-existent shoulders.

Filled with a sense of urgency, Daisy was preoccupied with steps she needed to take to stop the drug shipment. She would call someone for help, probably Lucas would be best so she would call him once she got to a straight stretch on the highway; she could take a shortcut to the airport, Old Murphy Road, to bypass downtown traffic; but she could not see a way to drop Louisa and Retta off anywhere on the way to the airport. They would have to stay with her.

CHAPTER 51

Reaching the Appalachian Highway Daisy sped as she turned toward Franklin, but soon left that to get back on the Old Murphy Highway. Bypassing the town center was the only way she could reach the airport in time. She had to slow down going up a hill behind a truck and she was finally able to call Lucas. It was about to go into voicemail when he answered.

"Daisy, where are you? I was expecting you to be home when Ed and I got here."

"We're on the way to the airport. Can you call Nathan for me?"

"Hold on a minute. Why are you going to the airport? Who's with you?"

"Retta and Louisa. Louisa told me that her husband is on the way to the airport to pick up a new shipment of heroin. Daddy, Joe Simpson is dead."

Her hands blanched as she squeezed the steering wheel of the Jeep to steady her nerves.

"Daisy, come home! This is too dangerous. I'll call Nathan, and Ben."

"We might be able to slow them down if we can get there before the plane can land. I have to try."

"Please listen to me. When you get to the airport, stay in your car until Ben and Nathan arrive. Can you at least promise me that?"

"I promise I'll try to wait."

"Just do it! These men are criminals who have murdered. They have nothing to lose by killing one more person."

"I understand, Dad. I've got to focus on driving now. I love you."

"I love you too."

At the top of the hill Daisy cut off her cell and passed the truck. Soon she reached the airport road and began to drive more cautiously. When the landing field was in sight, she pulled over and parked.

From the backseat Retta asked anxiously, "What can you see?"

"Not much," Daisy said. "Can you reach over the back and see if my backpack is there?"

"Here," Retta said lifting it high over to Daisy.

Daisy zipped it open and took out a pair of binoculars. Using them she scanned the field until she clearly saw the small group of men by the airport office.

"They're here. I see your husband, Louisa. But I don't see Jude."

After seeing Joe dead, Daisy had worried about Jude's safety.

"Don't worry, Louisa. I'll make sure Jude is safe."

Louisa looked horrified and shook her head.

"No," she began, "you didn't understand. Jude shot Joe. Jude killed his brother."

"Jude?" Daisy asked, already knowing the answer. Three dangerous men waited to pick up the heroin and probably other drugs, and she had to stop them. Jude came out of the office and spoke to his father.

"Wait. The plane is landing. The pilot must've waited until he knew that the men were there."

Daisy took some more shells from her backpack and shoved them in her pocket. She hung the binoculars around her neck and picked up the shotgun.

"Stay here. I want to get a better look."

Shrubs on one side of the road offered some cover. Daisy crept along and began to edge slowly closer to the airport. When she reached the end of the hedgerow, she lay flat on her belly. She and Jake had spent many an hour on their stomachs, waiting, watching silently for deer or bear to appear. They usually saw only squirrels or birds, but they were happy to have been in each other's company.

On this day Daisy was waiting to see something else, something dangerous, and she wished Jake were with her. Why hadn't she asked Lucas to call Jake, too?

CHAPTER

52

Daisy lay as still as she could in the tall weedy grasses at the end of the hedgerow. She clutched her shotgun by her right side. The plane had touched down and was circling around the runway until it could come to a full stop before the group of men.

Daisy knew she did not have much time. She would have to stand to fire at the men. She planned to fire a warning shot, just as Simpson had done on the first day when she had approached his cabin. If all went well, she could hold them until Nathan arrived. She trembled a bit. If only Jake were here, she thought.

Cautiously pushing herself up, Daisy sat with her back against the privet and focused on what Jake had taught her. The chamber was already loaded. She released the safety. She was ready. When the men walked to the small plane, Daisy dashed into place behind the office. She looked through a window to make sure it was empty, then she waited.

As the single cabin door opened, she held the grip firmly and loaded the chambers. Standing she placed the butt firmly against her chest. She would wait to engage the trigger. Where was Nathan?

She was surprised when Walker appeared at the door of the plane.

"The trip was very successful," he said to his son who had gone out to greet him.

They spoke while Simpson stood back. Daisy noticed that all the men were carrying firearms of one sort or another. Walker had a holstered handgun. The men still on the ground carried shotguns like Daisy. The pilot, who had followed Jude down the stairs, had a rifle.

Daisy stepped forward and squared off. But before she could fire her shot, the pilot saw her, took aim, and fired. Simultaneously someone tackled Daisy, pushed her to the ground, and fell on top of her. She looked over her shoulder and saw Jake grimacing at her.

"Hello, darlin'. This hasn't gone exactly as I'd figured," he winced.

Daisy could see that his right shoulder was bleeding. She pushed him off and began to drag him farther behind the airport office. Seeing the men running towards them, she laid him down as gently as she could and picked up her weapon. The shotgun was ready so all she had to do was to fire. She aimed at Jude and slowly squeezed the trigger. He fell.

Walker next.

"That was for Caleb," she cried out as he fell. "You never should have involved him in this."

The pilot had heard sirens nearing and stopped. He was running back to his plane.

Daisy looked around for Simpson. He was running back to the trucks. She called for him to stop and ran towards him. Then she saw Nathan.

Nathan had arrived with Ben and the other deputies and police.

"We'll take care of this now," he said.

He took her shotgun.

"That was very brave of you."

"I hardly knew what I was doing. I just knew they were coming to kill me and Jake."

"Speaking of Jake, an ambulance should be here soon. You okay, man?"

Jake nodded. Daisy fell to her knees by him.

"You just can't help interfering with my plans, can you?"

"Well," Jake said, "somebody has to, so it might as well be me, darlin'. We make a pretty good team, now don't we?"

CHAPTER 53

Daisy rode in the ambulance with Jake. He was treated in the emergency room and released with his arm in a sling. As his release papers were being prepared, Nathan arrived with the keys to Daisy's Jeep.

"All right?" he asked Jake.

Jake grinned. "Nothing serious. The bullet went straight through."

"Good deal."

Daisy marveled at the way the two men were talking to each other away from work situations. They seemed to speak in shorthand unlike the way Jake or her father spoke to her. Nathan turned to her.

"We took Simpson into custody and are trying to

determine the extent of his involvement. He doesn't seem to know much about the pipeline from Atlanta, but we'll keep working on him."

"Is that for publication?"

Nathan nodded.

"Just call the sheriff's office for an update."

"Thanks. I'm taking Jake home first and then go to the office to write it up."

CHAPTER 54

The Walkers' truck was in front of the cabin, but there was a strange car, a black Mercedes hatchback, parked alongside it. Daisy blocked both in with her Jeep. "I've come to check on Retta," she said when Jasmine opened the front door.

Jasmine waved her in. "Retta'll be glad to see you," she said. "She's still very upset, of course, about Dad."

A stranger stood in the doorway. He wore nice clothes, city clothes, all black down to his black Nikes. The black leather jacket said money to Daisy. Longish black hair added to his style. She had seen men dressed like this before in Asheville and Atlanta, even in Raleigh which was and is a very conservative city as far as fashion goes, sometimes on tourists, but never on men visiting in local homes.

"This is Christian, a friend from Atlanta. He had already planned to come for the weekend. Planning to come back for some deer hunting."

He smiled at Daisy, and his teeth were sparking white, his eyes were twinkling. This was the man Retta had mentioned.

"Daisy's the friend I told you about. She looked after Mama until I could get here."

"Hello. Have you known Jasmine very long?"

"Sure thing." Christian said. "We go way back."

Jasmine cut him off before he could say more.

"Retta's up and in the kitchen, if you want to go on back."

The back porch with its shed roof had been remodeled to accommodate a modern kitchen. A counter stretched under a long row of windows that filled a wall. Retta was putting French toast in one of the double ovens.

She walked over to hug Daisy.

"Have a seat, dear. I'll get us some coffee."

"Have you talked to Louisa? I'm going to see her on the way back."

"Just briefly. I'm going to ask her to come up here to stay until her husband is released, if he is released."

The smell of cinnamon began to fill the room and reminded Daisy that she had not eaten breakfast yet. She took a sip of the hot coffee and said, "Who is Christian?"

"Better stay clear of him. Bad news. I didn't realize that Jasmine knew him, too."

"Jasmine said he was her old friend. What kind of business?"

"Don't know. Nobody never discussed it with me. Walker always said he had something to do with investments. Men's business."

"They went deer hunting?"

"That's what they told me. They'd get their rifles and some gear and disappear for days. He left his cell at home so I couldn't call him, even if there were an emergency. They'd come back with venison wrapped for the freezer, and that's that."

"There's plenty of deer right around here. I wonder where they went."

"I quit asking. Walker just said it was a secret spot."

Jasmine and Christian entered the room.

"Do I smell French toast? Bacon to go with it?" Jasmine said. "Daisy, pull up a chair and stay for breakfast."

"Thanks, but I've got to get to work."

Christian walked over, grabbed Daisy's arm and began to direct her towards the door.

"I can see myself out."

"Pero no!" Christian said. "A gentleman always escorts a lady such as yourself."

He walked her to her car and opened the door. He said, "Until next time, chica," and winked at her. Daisy shuddered as he closed the door.

The car doors had locked automatically when she switched on the ignition, but she doublechecked before starting it, did a y-turn, and left.

As she drove carefully down the rutted gravel road, trying to avoid potholes created by the recent storms, she thought about Walker and Christian. An unlikely pair. What kind of investments, I wonder? Could Christian really be a stockbroker? How did Jasmine fit in? She turned her full attention to the road and drove toward the Ruby Mine and Louisa.

CHAPTER 55

Louisa was nowhere to be seen when Daisy entered the store. She imagined Louisa was upstairs, perhaps sleeping after the traumatic events. She was about to call out and go upstairs but heard a car door slam out front. It was the black Mercedes.

Christian burst into the room. He paused and closed the door behind him, then he drew a knife from his jacket pocket.

"Chiquita, you left before we had a chance to talk. I want to know you better."

Daisy drew herself up and screwed up her courage.

"I know everything about you that I need to know."

Christian let out a malevolent laugh then cursed under his breath.

"Do you now?"

As he inched closer with the knife pointed at her, she struggled to stay calm.

"You're nothing but a low-life drug dealer, small fish in the scheme of things."

"Certainly, your mother thought the same."

"My mother?"

"Si, you know, as I look at you now, I realize, you look just like your mother."

The sound of another car door slamming shut distracted Christian long enough for Daisy to attack. She placed a lucky kick to knock the knife from his hand and was preparing to tackle him when Jasmine came through the door and fired.

"Patron," he whispered as he fell.

Daisy rushed to him. She pressed on the wound made by Jasmine's gun and said, "Don't die now. What about my mother?'

"Now you'll never know…."

He was dead.

"Daisy, are you okay?"

"Why did you shoot him? He was just about to tell me how he knew my mother."

She was gazing at her hands covered with Christian's blood when Louisa came down the stairs.

"Daisy! Jasmine! What's happened? Are you okay?"

Daisy stood up and stared.

CHAPTER 56

It was about a week later before Jake and Daisy were able to return to the Walker place. Daisy made daily visits to the Smiths' farm. At first, she helped Jake's mother with household chores and looked after Jake. She changed the dressing twice a day and made sure he took the antibiotics and painkillers that he had been prescribed at the right time and dosage.

The wound to Jake's arm turned out to be superficial and healed quickly. Friday afternoon Daisy drove him to the doctor's office. The doctor was pleased when he took a look and said, "Jake, you're doing better than I thought you would. You must have had a good nurse."

He winked at Daisy.

"You no longer need the bandages or sling. Finish

the course of antibiotics. You can use the Nurofen as needed. I'll call in a prescription for one more refill, but you could use over-the-counter ibuprofen if the pain isn't too bad. There's no long-term damage to the muscles that I can see, but your arm might be tender for a while, as the muscles continue to heal."

Daisy drove Jake home. "What are your plans for the weekend?"

"I've got to get back in the garden. I imagine I've got a lot of weeding to do. Greens should be ready to pick."

"I'll come by in the morning."

"Suit yourself, Nurse McLaren," Jake winked at her.

"Eff you!"

Daisy drove straight home and went directly into the big house. Lucas was once again seated at the round table where they had shared so many meals, and Ed was slicing vegetables for a salad. Daisy hugged them both.

"I guess you want me to do the salad again," she said to Ed.

"I won't say no if you ask to fix it."

Daisy took over the salad prep duties and rather than slicing she commenced by chopping finely for a chopped salad like she had eaten at the California Pizza Kitchen at Southpoint in Durham. In the refrigerator she found deli ham and mozzarella cheese. She mixed oil, vinegar, and Italian herbs in the large wooden bowl, dumped in the chopped ingredients, and tossed.

Ed reappeared with grilled chicken basted with barbecue sauce from the other side of the great room. He had been working at the grill on the patio outside that side of the house. He had already placed grilled bread in a basket and wrapped in a clean napkin on the table.

"Chow time," he said.

Daisy carried the salad over, and everyone was happy to dig in.

"If there are leftovers, I'd like to carry some to Jake and his mom tomorrow."

"How is he doing?"

"Better, but he plans to get back to work on their garden and I don't want him to overdo it. I'm going to help him whether he wants my help or not. I'll probably stay over if we work late."

The next morning Daisy fed Rescue, packed an overnight bag, and hurried back to Jake's farm. He and his mom were having a hearty breakfast oatmeal, cheese omelets, and toast.

"Do you want some oatmeal, Daisy? There's plenty left?"

"No thank you, Mrs. Smith."

"Now please call me Clemmie."

"Okay Clemmie. I've brought some barbecued chicken and chopped salad we had for dinner. Can I put it in your fridge?"

"Thank you, dear."

Daisy put the food away and then said, "I have a bag in the car in case we work late, and I need to stay over. Is that okay?"

Jake's mother nodded.

"Let's get this show on the road, darlin', if you're

insisting on getting in my way."

Daisy let it roll off her and went outside. Suzie Q was waiting for them, and this time went straight to Daisy and put her paws on her shoulders. Once she settled into a good position, she planted sloppy kisses all over Daisy's face. Daisy giggled as she grabbed the hound's paws and pushed the Redbone hound to the ground. "Sit!" To her surprise the dog obeyed.

"Come on Suzie." Jake barked, and she leaped to her feet and pranced toward the garden at his heels. She obviously adored her master. Abandoned by both, Daisy followed along.

The tools were already in the vegetable patch. Jake handed her a hoe. "Chop at the weeds between the rows."

Suzie Q had settled down at the head of the row where Jake was working. He pinched off the lower leaves off the turnip greens and pushed them down into a plastic grocery bag from Walmart. He pulled the whole plant when a found a root large enough to cook.

Daisy continued to clear the weeds as Jake harvested the vegetables that were ready. After he picked the last of the vine-ripened tomatoes, he stood for a while and watched Daisy hard at work. When she paused to wipe her sweaty brow, she saw Jake. His usual smirk had been replaced with a look best described as tender. "What?" Daisy asked.

"You missed some." Jake motioned above his right eyebrow. "The other one!" he said as Daisy rubbed above her left eyebrow.

"Let's tote all this in. It must be time for lunch."

Jake's mother had prepared another inviting lunch spread. This time one platter in the center held homemade bread, sliced for sandwiches. The other platter contained pimiento and cheese, sliced baked chicken, sliced tomatoes, and lettuce.

"We'll have your chicken and salad this evening."

The rest of the weekend followed the same pattern. She and Jake would rise early and get to work on the weeding between the plants and enjoy delicious meals together. In the evenings they would sit in rocking chairs on the front porch with Suzie Q and talk about the friends they knew as kids.

On Sunday night Daisy packed her things to return to her apartment in town. Her thoughts returned to Jasmine; when Jake helped her carry her bags to the Jeep, she brought up her concerns.

"You know, I really thought that Jasmine was a part of it. Especially after Keira told Lexie that she had seen Jasmine in town at the time of the crash. If she weren't a part of the smuggling, then why wouldn't she stay with Retta and Walker, or at the very least let them know she was in town? It was also very weird that Keira disappeared after telling me about Jasmine."

"Keira left a note saying she had gone to Asheville for a new job. And why would she have shot Christian if she was working with him? She saved your life. It doesn't make any sense. You're seeing mystery where there isn't any."

"I suppose. What could he have meant when he

said 'patron'? He was whispering but I'm pretty sure that was the word."

"I don't know much Spanish, but maybe he said 'puta.' That's one word I know that I might say if I were looking at someone pointing a gun at me."

"Maybe. I better go. Back to work tomorrow."

CHAPTER 57

Monday morning brought an even more dazzling autumn day. Brilliant reds, oranges, yellows, and golds adorned the trees. The falling leaves were scattering a carpet on the forest floor. Intermittent breezes were gently peeling them away and sending them fluttering in the air.

Daisy rose early and went to her apartment to change clothes. Rescue's bowls contained water and kibble, so she had been well-cared for over the weekend. In the bedroom she was wreathed upon Daisy's pillow, which she usually treated more respectfully. The small cat had strewn Daisy's pens and pencils helter-skelter around the bedroom. Papers and paperbacks had been gnawed at enough to be unusable. She opened one eye briefly and quickly closed it. Had the great room been wrecked in the same fashion Daisy would have thought intruders had been in again.

"Out of the closet at last. Missed me, did you?" she said. "A little angry as well? That's still no reason to show off like this. There's always the Appalachian Animal Rescue Center that I could call for you."

Daisy stretched out sideways on the bed to pet Rescue. The cat got up and stretched out herself, then got in a downward dog position before finally sitting next to Daisy's face and touching it gently with one paw.

"I guess you're a keeper. Not every woman is lucky enough to have a watch cat! What do you say we get some breakfast?" Rescue mewed, and Daisy picked her up and carried her to the kitchen.

She changed Rescue's water and to celebrate the end of this traumatic period in their lives she opened a can of salmon. Everything was back to normal. Daisy breathed a sigh of relief at enjoying the ordinariness of their lives this morning.

Ed had stocked her refrigerator and pantry shelf with more food than Daisy needed, and Daisy took advantage of this to prepare a breakfast equal to Ed's famous brunches. Her waffle was frozen, not homemade, but she drenched it in real maple syrup. She made a waffle with gruyere cheese and mushrooms, and added a small bowl of mixed fruit, consisting of orange sections, pineapple chunks, and sliced pears, from a batch Ed provided.

Her cell phone chimed as she was finishing her

breakfast.

"Daisy, it's Retta. I hope I didn't wake you."

"No, ma'am."

"I don't feel we've thanked you properly for everything you did to help us."

"It was nothing."

"Come now. No need for false modesty. Louisa and I would like you and Jake to have lunch with us today. Can you come around noon?"

"Actually, we were already planning to come by to check on y'all. I'll ask Jake about the time and give you a call if he can't make it then."

Daisy confirmed the lunch date with Jake. She took a long hot shower. Her short hair was already in need of a trim, too long to spike it up with gel. She fixed it as best she could and put on some basic make-up—lipstick, blush, and mascara—and went to Lucas's.

The house was quietly empty. Daisy had enjoyed Retta's motherly company and was excited to be seeing her again. She sat for a while reading the Sunday *Atlanta Journal-Constitution* left on the table. The front page contained an article, lower right-hand corner, about the previous Monday's incident. Neither Daisy nor Jake was mentioned by name. Most of the quotes were attributed to the sheriff, with a few others from townspeople expressing shock that such things had been happening in Franklin.

Shortly before noon Daisy picked Jake up from work at Drake Enterprises and they drove out the Appalachian Highway to Ruby Mine Road where it all had begun. Jake tuned the radio to the local station that was doing the morning call-in show where people could buy, sell, or barter all kinds of items or jobs.

They both turned to glance at the Simpson Ruby Mine office as they drove by.

"Come on in," said Retta as she greeted them at the door.

Louisa was already seated at the table nursing a sweet tea. In the center of the table were a large salad bowl and a breadbasket with a red-checked cloth napkin wrapped around bread that had just come out of the oven. Retta carried bowls of soup from the counter to the table and joined them.

"I thought you wouldn't want a heavy meal since you're back at work today."

They made small talk as they ate, inquiring about each other's health, discussing how Louisa and Retta were settling in together.

"I thought Jasmine would be here," Daisy said. "I didn't get to thank her for rescuing me from Christian."

"She left that same afternoon," Retta said. "She's always so busy. I had hoped she would stay on a bit to help Louisa move in, but she couldn't."

"Did she tell you how she knew him?"

"She met him through a friend and didn't know him well. She was so shocked and sorry for what he tried to do to you. Thank God she came when she did."

Daisy nodded. When they had finished eating, Retta left the table and returned with a small tin box.

"As I read your story about de Soto and Chualiah

in the paper, I thought I should show you this."

She opened the box and carefully removed and place on the table an assortment of rubies, emeralds, sapphires, pearls, glass beads, a mother-of-pearl hair comb, and several gold, copper, and silver Spanish coins. She fingered them tenderly as rare treasures.

"These have been in my family for generations. My mother gave them to me when I married. I should give them to Jasmine, but she hasn't gotten married and doesn't seem interested in our history."

"They're so beautiful," Daisy said. The gemstones had not been cut but they had been handled so many times through the centuries that they glistened and seemed to shine from a light within.

"I don't know exactly when my ancestors made their way to the area around Franklin, and I never heard about an attack on the Spaniards at the Nikwasi Mound. But these have been passed down from mother to oldest daughter along with the legend about Chualiah outsmarting and finally escaping from de Soto in these Appalachian Mountains."

EPILOGUE

"Have you been doing your deep breathing every day?"

Daisy leaned back into a comfortable blue armchair across from Dr. Ammons and stared at the three spider plants hung across the picture window to the patio. Had she looked in the other direction she could have stared at an aquarium filled with iridescent tetras.

"I practice at night when I'm in bed. It helps me fall asleep."

"Good. I'm glad you can see that focusing on your breath can derail obsessive thoughts that can keep you awake at night."

Neither spoke for a few moments. Dr. Ammons became her psychotherapist when she returned to Franklin after her mother's death. She had been given an anti-anxiety medication at the UNC Hospital in Chapel Hill when she first received the news about the accident. She weaned Daisy off that medication but kept her on the antidepressant she had already been prescribed.

"I keep seeing Jake shot and then the men, Walker and Jude falling when I shot them."

"You saved Jake's life, and your own. Jake has almost fully recovered. You did what you had to do."

"I guess. I mean, I know you are right. It's just that killing a person, two men. I can still see their faces as I shot them. And Jake wounded, bleeding beside me. I don't think any of that would've happened if I had listened to everyone. If I had stayed out of it. Let the sheriff take care of it."

Uncontrollable sobs poured from Daisy. Dr. Ammons said nothing and let her cry.

Dr. Ammons typed notes into the iPad she held in her hands. She tapped Enter and handed Daisy a Kleenex.

"This is the first time you have been able to say out loud what happened that day and how it made you feel. I know how very upsetting it is. Although you may not realize it, this is a huge breakthrough."

Daisy looked at her psychiatrist without truly comprehending what she had said. The doctor typed some more into the iPad.

"I want you to come in three times a week for the next two weeks. I think we can make real progress in that time. Then the following week, we'll look at your situation again and perhaps bring Lucas in for a family therapy session. How does that sound?"

"It sounds good if you really think that would help. I can't go on having these thoughts every night." Daisy sniffled into the Kleenex.

"Between now and then I want you to continue with the deep breathing. You can set up the appointments on your way out. You can be very proud of yourself. You're the one doing the hard work; I'm simply your guide."

Daisy felt lighter as she left the office and walked to her Jeep. She chose to believe Dr. Ammons and could see a good future ahead.

The series of articles she wrote about the events of the past months had been bought by the *Raleigh News & Observer* for the Sunday edition and was featured on the website. The editor-in-chief had been so impressed that he invited her to come in to interview for a staff position. Unready to accept the offer she was nevertheless flattered. Lucas had advised her to reply that she had other commitments but that she would get back in touch once she was free to consider other employment.

The sun was glowing hot in a cloudless Carolina blue sky. As Daisy drove away from the medical building, she called Jake to find out what he wanted to do for the Fourth of July.

Acknowledgements

Writing this book during the Coronavirus (COVID-19) Pandemic of 2020-2021 was challenging, but in the enforced isolation I could not make any excuse for not completing this, my first mystery.

My family treasured words and books. We had a modest bookcase in our dining room; I can see myself seated on the floor selecting the next book to read. I can see myself going down the steps to the basement of the original town library, I suppose to the children's section. I see myself in the adult section of the new library; I remember my father hauling me over to meet Miss Eudora Welty in front of that library.

So first I must thank my family, my late parents, Gladys and Ernest, and brother Ed; my sister Mary who encouraged me to stay at it and finish the book and who bragged to her friends as the end neared; my brother Calvin, one of the great Southern storytellers whose gift is all-too-often unsung. I especially gives thanks for my son and daughter-in-law who have provided for all my needs and made sure that I was healthy and safe. Thanks to my friends Anne, Lynn, Jane, and Kay for their encouragement. Thanks to our cats, the rescued sisters Emily and Penny without whom the joy of writing and one plot point would be absent.

Writing is a solitary endeavor but, in addition to family and friends, a community of writers contributed to this project. Starting with the Memoir Writing Group at the Franklin NC Senior Center, Debbie who met with me in a room at the library until the virus made that impossible, Bruce and the Highlands NC writing group that meets in person and now by ZOOM every Tuesday, other ZOOM meetings with Sisters in Crime national organization and Atlanta and TriangleNC Chapters, and finally, ZOOM and webinar classes with Jane Cleland, Paula Munier, and Gina Panettieri.

Most research had to be done with the help of Mr. Google and Ms. Wiki, but I was fortunate to have met Mike Ayers, currently the Director of Georgia's Criminal Justice Coordinating Council. As the GBI Agent in Charge of the Athens GA office, he graciously took me on a tour of the facilities; provided tips on how agents work in the real world, especially that they conduct interviews in the field rather than in small rooms with tape recorders; and shared an example from his career of how truth is indeed stranger than fiction. That story appears in the mystery as a major turning point, and I will be eternally grateful to him for sharing that as one professional to another.

An enormous shout out to my #5amwritersclub. I might not join them each morning at five, but they are a constant reminder to write every day. Cheers to them and groups like them.

And thank you, Dear Reader, for picking up and reading my humble addition to the vast collection of mysteries.

About the Author

Ruth McCoy drew the inspiration for this thrilling mystery from her home in the mountains surrounding the small community of Franklin, North Carolina. She is a graduate of the University of North Carolina at Chapel Hill where she majored in English and Basketball.

Made in the USA
Columbia, SC
17 September 2021

45671187R00148